CREATION SCIENCE CLUB

Challenging Dr. E.V. Lution

John and Lisa Fox

Challenging Dr. E.V. Lution
The Creation Science Club: Book 2
by John and Lisa Fox

First printing: January 2016

ISBN 978-1-942773-01-6
Cover design: BookFuel
Design and layout: BookFuel
Style and proofreading: Dr. Robert Carter and Lita Cosner

Published by:

CREATION BOOK PUBLISHERS

Creation Book Publishers
P.O. Box 350
Powder Springs, GA, 30127, USA.
Phone: 1-800-616-1264
creationbookpublishers.com

We dedicate this book
to the memory of
William James Rankin,
and to his family,
with our love.

We also want to thank:

Buddy Davis, whose creation music ministry and dinosaur sculpting first inspired us to dig deeper into the truth,

Jonathan Sarfati, who has written books to refute the endless barrage of evolution's 'overwhelming evidence' coming at us from every side,

Creation Ministries International, for providing us all with various resources and an endless supply of 'scientific stones of truth' for our slings.

With special gratitude to Dr. Robert Carter, Lita Cosner, and others at CMI for taking the time to review this book.

*Note: If any errors or misuse of terms or facts
occur in this series, these mistakes are solely
the responsibility of the authors.

PART 1

The Age of the Dinosaurs

CHAPTER 1

With squeaks and squeals of delight, Pudgy hurried from one plant on the hillside to the next. Each plant seemed more delicious than the last. The young triceratops paused only for a moment to look back at the goats bawling at him through the hole he had made in the barnyard fence. Hurrying on to the next green plant, he wondered why they didn't just come and enjoy the feast with him. You see, to Pudgy, food equaled good. So, if being out of his owner's yard meant more food, then being out of the yard was good. Obviously, Pudgy was not the sharpest tool in the shed.

Further up the hill, cold eyes turned toward the sounds coming from below. Lowering itself onto all fours, the creature crept up behind a pile of rocks left by the farmer. Its eyes narrowed as they locked onto its prey, its keen mind quickly forming a plan. Then the predator advanced—step by step, slowly closing the gap between itself and Pudgy. Soon its stomach would be full.

Pudgy could hear all the farm animals sending urgent warnings from down in the yard. With an impatient grunt, he spun around to see what all the ruckus was about. In an instant, every nerve in his body came tingling to life, for he found himself facing the most feared beast of the countryside—a dragon. Pudgy backed away and instinctively lowered his large head.

The dragon merely sneered. Pudgy's horns were still nothing but harmless nubs. With a hiss, the creature stood up on its hind legs. It was unusual to find a small triceratops all alone, without the protection of its large three-horned parents. The large sickle-like claws, one on each of the velociraptor's back feet, raised up menacingly—ready for action. This would be quick and easy.

But suddenly, from behind, the beast felt a sharp pain. Gnashing its teeth, it spun to face its attacker. Then the dragon itself began to back away. There was only one thing this beast feared—man. The farmer put another stone in his slingshot and made contact with the raptor's neck. Shrieking and growling, it continued to back away.

Seeing the chance for escape, Pudgy ran as fast as his short legs would carry him—back toward the safety of the farmyard. The dragon was enraged by the sight of its meal getting away. Rising to its full height, it raced toward the man. Jumping high into the air, the velociraptor thrust a deadly sickle claw toward the man's chest. The farmer, however, was prepared. He had a long, strong spear raised and ready to meet the beast.

Then, out of nowhere, a four-wheel-drive jeep appeared. The blond-haired driver honked the jeep's horn and shouted, "Come on, you three! We've got to get back to the cabin if we're gonna get anything done tonight."

The velociraptor immediately dropped down, sprawling ungracefully on its backside. Pudgy stopped running and stood up on his hind legs. The farmer lowered his spear and reached up to remove his *R.M.—Reality Morphing*—glasses. "Ummm...sure, Billy," he called. "We're coming." David

Avila and Darin and Abel Tadue each blinked a few times in order to refocus on their present reality, then headed down to the waiting jeep.

As they drove out of Green Trees Park, Billy shushed his noisy friends and pointed out into the middle of some autumn-colored fields. A group of deer stood nearly invisible among the meadow grass. "See, the deer have traded in their summer clothes for winter coats. They blend nearly perfectly with all the colors of winter. Now they can hide simply by staying still."

"Wow!" David whispered. "I guess God thought of everything."

Billy smiled. "Well, David, everything we look at—from the dandelion to the oak, from the mouse to the whale—they all preach the awesome power of their Creator."

David settled back into his seat with an unhappy sigh. "That's sure not what Dr. E. V. Lution, Ph.D. times three, would say."

Then, out of the dusky air, Dr. Lution himself responded, "David, it is my job to convince you that the impossible is possible and that the ridiculous is right." Abel had been practicing Dr. Lution's voice and had done such a convincing job that everyone laughed out loud, spooking the group of deer. For a minute, they just watched the small herd bound off with their large white flags waving.

Then Billy put the jeep into drive and started down the road. "David, I know it's discouraging that Miss Lution got fired right when she was joining creation's side. But look at it this way, now we have a chance to show her father the Truth, too."

David's face brightened a bit. "Yeah, that's true. I mean, who would've thought we'd convince Miss Lution that the Bible is better science than evolution. But we did! Maybe Dr. Lution will come to see the real scientific evidence for biblical creation, too."

Soon, the jeep was turning off Pioneer Road and on its way up Maple Hill, toward a spacious cabin now quite visible among the leafless November trees.

This cabin is the office and workshop of this small group of scientists who call themselves the Creation Science Club. At the beginning of the school year, Billy, Darin, and Abel had decided to volunteer as science tutors for Darwin Middle School's honors science students.

There, the three of them had joined up with the class' outspokenly Christian student, David Avila. Together, they scaled the Grand Canyon, swam the waters of Galápagos, and hiked Yellowstone National Park in order to provide convincing evidence that the Bible's explanation of creation is more scientific (and believable) than evolution.

****

As soon as Billy parked, Darin and Abel hopped out and ran toward the cabin whispering and giggling. Then, Abel threw open the cabin door and shouted in a familiar cartoonish voice, "Wilma, I'm home! And, I've brought guests. How about bringin' us some snacks." At this, Darin started running in circles, yipping and yapping and making a silly attempt at wagging his nonexistent tail.

When Darin ran yipping his way, David was quick to jump behind the protection of a nearby chair. But Darin leaped right onto the chair and prepared himself for an enthusiastic attack.

"Down, Dino!" Abel commanded in his borrowed voice. Then he walked over to David, slapped him on the back, and said, "So, here you are visiting Bedrock. I guess you decided you could get the best scoop on dinosaurs from those of us who actually live with them, huh?"

David was smiling, but kept a suspicious eye on Darin, who was crouched down as if ready to spring. "So, who are you guys supposed to be?"

Darin growled and continued his high-pitched barking. Abel slapped David on the back again. "Well, I'm Fred Flintstone, of course. And, obviously, this is my little pet dinosaur, Dino."

Then Darin spoke up. "We're just demonstrating that dinosaurs and people really *did* exist together. You know, that's what your next science report is about—when dinosaurs existed."

David rolled his eyes and flopped onto the couch. "Thanks, guys. But, I think Dr. Lution's gonna need more convincing evidence than *The Flintstones*. I mean, yesterday he had all of us honors kids stay after school to watch a *two-hour* video of different trips he's taken to all sorts of museums and parks and dino-digs and university laboratories. That video must have said, 'dinosaurs have been extinct for over 60 million years' at least *60 million times*. No way is Dr. Lution gonna believe people and dinosaurs existed together."

With a quick leap, Darin flew off his chair and landed in front of David's slouching figure. Then, grabbing up the DVD remote, he raised his face to the cabin ceiling and howled, "Yabba-dabba-doo! Have we got a show for you!"

Abel, a.k.a. Fred, glanced around, put his hands on his hips and shouted, "Wilma, where are those snacks?"

On cue, Billy came into the room carrying a tray of apple slices, pretzels, and a bowl full of grapes. But, before putting the tray down, he made it very clear. "Anyone who calls me *Wilma* gets to ride home on the jeep's bumper!"

Then, with a click of the remote, the TV screen lit up with the scene of a raft swaying and rocking along a river shore. Water splashed up on the camera lens and different voices were shouting in the background. Up the river, the group was out of their rafts and trudging through the Alaskan summer's semi-frozen mud.

The next scene was of the men digging in a hillside. It was a messy job, but it wasn't long before someone shouted and the camera focused in on him. A man with a very red nose held a large piece of bone up to the screen. He shouted, "Check it out! I got it out of the permafrost—still frozen. And, based on its light weight, it's probably unfossilized!"

David turned to look at Billy. "What is it? Why are they so excited?"

Darin paused the video while Billy explained. "A team of creation scientists went up to Alaska and found unfossilized dinosaur bones."

"No way! I didn't know there were any dinosaur bones that weren't fossilized."

Abel grabbed the remote from Darin. "Watch and learn," he said, restarting the video. The scene changed to a laboratory where a paleontologist was explaining a recent fossil find. "These are Lambeosaurus bones. Notice the soft tissue material that shows in the cross-section cut of this bone."

David commented, "Dr. Lution's video sure didn't talk about this."

The next scene was an archeologist at a dinosaur dig site examining a large, broken fossil. "I can't believe there is soft, even elastic, tissue in the thigh bone of this T-Rex. There even appears to be blood vessels, if I'm not mistaken!"

David responded, "Is he saying that's *dinosaur blood!* Why aren't we being told this kind of stuff at school?"

"This next guy will tell you why, David-dude," Darin answered.

The video continued with a well-known creation speaker. "For many years, we've been told that dinosaur fossils are millions of years old. However, strong scientific evidence seems to show that soft tissue and blood vessels cannot survive for millions of years. So, these recent fossil discoveries challenge evolution's firm belief in millions of years. The possibility that totally unfossilized dinosaur bones have been found in the permafrost of Alaska…"

David grabbed the remote from Abel and paused the DVD again. His eyes sparkled with adventure. "Why don't we all go to Alaska? Why don't we go get our own unfossilized bones? No way can Dr. Lution argue with unfossilized dinosaur bones. Doesn't it sound like great fun?"

"Great fun?" Darin burst out emphatically. "Billions of giant, man-eating mosquitoes, freezing winds, prowling grizzly bears, quicksand, and absoluto-like-super-total exhaustion are *not* my idea of great fun."

"What's the matter, Dino?" Fred Flintstone taunted. "You afraid of a few little mosquitoes?"

As Darin started throwing pretzels at Abel, Billy broke in. "Don't worry, Darin. It's much too cold to venture up into Alaska this time of year. But…I was thinking about somewhere warmer. Somewhere…like…Argentina."

David's face shifted to a look of uncertainty. "Argentina? Are there unfossilized dinosaur bones down in Argentina?"

"Well…I can't promise unfossilized bones. But, you have to realize that unfossilized bones are only one of several clues you can find at a dino-dig that show dinosaurs certainly didn't live millions of years ago."

David's smile returned. "Cool! Then we're going to a dino-dig?"

"That's the plan, if your parents agree. A couple colleagues of mine are working at a dig in the Patagonia region. Most of their workers will be taking the week of Thanksgiving off, so they said they could use all the help they could get."

"Thanksgiving?" David asked in surprise. "But, this report is due before Thanksgiving Break."

"That's okay, David," Billy assured him. "We're already finding enough good information for this report. I'm sure Argentina will be perfect for your next report."

Then Billy turned to Darin who was preparing to launch himself at Abel. "Down, Dino! We've got to finish up this DVD so we can get David home by 8:30. Besides, Carmen is expecting me by 9:00."

"Translation:" Darin said in a know-it-all tone, "Mrs. Carmen has made a fresh batch of cookies, and Billy wants to have a couple for bedtime snack."

"Close," Billy admitted. "Only, its apple muffins. She said they'd be out of the oven at 9:00 sharp."

David rubbed his stomach. "Mmm…sounds good. But my mama said she'd be saving me a double serving of flan for my bedtime snack."

"Oooh, flan!" Billy and Abel said together.

"However," Darin smiled smugly, "Abel and I have no reason to be jealous, since Mom made the world's most fantabulous pumpkin rolls last night. We'll be eating the second one tonight."

"Okay, okay," Billy laughed. "For now, we'd better just finish up this DVD."

Then, turning to David, he said, "This next section is where we showed Dr. Theodore Veritas some of this same evidence."

The screen showed the face of Dr. Veritas watching a slide show of various fossil finds. As he listened to Billy's narration, Dr. Veritas ran his fingers through his hair and pulled at his beard.

"Look, Ted," Billy concluded in the video, "science seems to show that the blood cells and soft tissue that have been found in some dinosaur bones cannot have existed for millions of years. The only reasonable conclusion is that these bones are not millions, but only thousands of years old. This is compatible with the timeline given in the Bible."

Dr. Veritas leaned back in his chair with a heavy sigh. Shaking his head, he said, "Billy, my friend, I'm afraid you can't change generations of evolutionary thinking and billions of dollars of evolutionary research just by displaying a few supposedly unfossilized bones."

Back at Maple Hill cabin, Abel smirked and said slowly, "Yab-ba-dab-ba-doo! We-are-sure-gonna-show-you!"

CHAPTER 2

That next Saturday, David and the gang spent the morning at *The Library of Secular Science* gathering books on the evolutionists' ideas of the age of the dinosaurs. Seated in the midst of piles and stacks of books, they discovered Jack and Jill Hill—friends of David from his honors science class. Jill looked frustrated, and Jack looked disgusted.

David stepped in, through, and over all the books. "Hey, Jack! How's it going, Jill?" he whispered with a smile. "Looks like you've got the whole dinosaur section pulled out."

Jill rolled her eyes. "Nope, this is just the last third of them. This library is stocked to the hilt with dinosaur books!"

Jack shut a nicely illustrated book with a vicious bang. "We've spent the last three evenings here trying to find even one book that doesn't say dinosaurs are millions of years old." With an exasperated sigh, Jack waved his hand toward all the books around them and said, "Not one! It's so frustrating!"

Jill looked toward Billy with tears in her eyes. "You know, Mr. James, our dad was so encouraged and excited to hear how real science backs up the truth of the Bible. But then Dr. Lution throws this dinosaur thing at us." Shaking her head she added, "It's too bad the Bible doesn't talk about dinosaurs."

Abel looked at Darin and winked. Then, raising his face to the glass ceiling, he let loose with a "Yabba-dabba-doo! Have we got good news for you!"

A surprised, and somewhat peeved, librarian looked out from the creatively decorated window to the children's reading section of the library. But, as soon as the woman saw who had been causing the disturbance, her scowl relaxed into a smile. "I should have known it was you guys! Remember, use your library voices."

"Good morning, Miss Abbi," Darin and Abel said together, waving to their friend. Then they raced each other to see who got to go first through the slide tunnel that acted as the more interesting entrance to the kids' space.

A group of young children squealed and giggled as Darin and Abel came sprawling head-first off the slide in front of them. Abel looked a bit embarrassed. "Gee, Miss Abbi, you didn't tell us it was story hour."

But Darin just sat down by one of the kids and whispered excitedly, "Oh, boy, what story is she reading?"

Just then, Billy and the others entered the story room through the more conventional door. All the children cheered. They loved Billy's stories. Miss Abigail Informed laughed and said, "Well, Mr. James, today we were reading stories about dragons. Do you have any stories for us about dragons?"

Billy took a seat and turned to the children. "Dragons are some of the most fascinating creatures that ever existed. In fact," he said, nodding toward Jack and Jill, "my friends and I were just talking about when dragons walked the earth."

One little girl, about five, cocked her head to the side and said with a giggle, "Aw, Mr. James, sir, dragons aren't for real."

Billy's face was full of shock and mischief as he answered, "Now, who told you that?" Then he turned to the other children and asked, "Who here has heard of dinosaurs?" All the children raised their hands. "Yep," he continued, "and we all know that dinosaurs existed. People find their bones all the time, and we see 'em in the museums."

"Now, Mr. James," Miss Informed said cautiously, "you're not going to say that dinosaurs and dragons are the same thing, are you? I mean, dragons are mythological creatures from the medieval times. But dinosaurs died out millions of years before people were even around."

Again, Billy's face was a picture of shock and mischief as he asked, "Now, Miss Abbi, who told you that?"

Leaning forward, Billy smiled into the eyes of the eager children before him. "You know what? I'll bet that all of you have heard of the most famous dinosaur book ever. Who here can tell me what it is?"

"*Land Before Time!*" a boy shouted enthusiastically.

Billy pointed at the boy and said, "That's a great guess, but it's not what I'm looking for. Anyone else have a guess?"

"*Dinosaur Island*," another boy tried.

Billy sat back a bit. "Hmmm, another good guess. Still not what I had in mind. Let's see, now…who here went to church last Sunday?" Most of the children raised their hands. "Okay, then, what book did you read at church?"

The girl next to Abel answered shyly, "My Sunday School teacher had me read a verse out of the Bible."

"That's it!" Billy laughed. "That's the book I'm talking about—the most famous book *ever* that talks about dinosaurs is the Bible. If we just…"

Jack interrupted, "Mr. James—Billy—did you say dinosaurs are mentioned in the *Bible*?" Then, he turned to Jill excitedly. "He said dinosaurs *are* in the Bible. This is great!"

Miss Informed looked very surprised. "Really? I mean, in the regular old *Holy Bible*?"

Abel laughed. "Yep! In the really and true Holy Bible. The book of Job mentions a couple of possible dinosaurs. You know, Job is considered to be one of the most ancient books of the Bible. Anyway, Job chapter 40 describes this massive creature called Behemoth. And, if you look at the description, it really sounds like some sort of sauropod—you know, like a brachiosaurus or an apatosaurus."

Miss Informed drew her eyebrows down and shook her head. "If the Bible *really* mentions dinosaur-like creatures, why weren't we told about this? I mean, everything I've ever read or heard says that dinosaurs were extinct millions of years before people came into the picture."

Abel went over and patted the librarian on the shoulder in a comforting sort of way. She caught onto his point and laughed. "I know, I know. I guess I've been *misinformed*!"

The children began to get impatient, and a bold little boy called out, "Come on, Mr. Billy, tell us a story!"

Billy laughed and said, "Okay, okay. I've got the perfect story. But, I think you bigger kids better get out of here and get your research done while I entertain our little friends in here." David, Jack, and Jill went whispering excitedly out of kids' space.

"You know," David said as he picked up an arm load of books to put back on the shelves, "dinosaur-like creatures aren't only mentioned in the book of Job. If you use the King James Version, the word *dragon* is used in other books, too—like, Psalms and some of the prophets."

Jill almost danced around the piles of dinosaur books. "Jack, I just can't wait to get home and show Dad that there could be for-real dinosaurs in the Bible!"

****

Sitting in Billy's jeep out in Biggie Burger's parking lot, Darin had his coat hood up and the string pulled so tight that only his nose poked through the remaining hole. "Man, Billy," Darin complained, "you need to get a hardtop cover for this thing. This soft top doesn't keep the cold out at all."

"Cheer up, Dino!" Abel joked. "A giant plate of Mr. Biggie's hot and spicy pterodactyl wings should warm you right up."

Everyone hopped out of the jeep. But, as Darin tried to take his hood off, he ran into the car next to them. "Hey!" he shouted in alarm. "My hood string is tied in a knot. I'm stuck in my hood and I can't get out. Heee-yelp!"

David hurried into Biggie Burgers to get out of the cold while Abel and Billy tried to get Darin out of his hood. Heading toward the club's favorite booth, David came face to face with Dr. E. V. Lution himself. Both David and Dr. Lution looked surprised to see each other. David worked up his courage and said in a friendly sort of way, "Uh, Hi, Dr. Lution, sir."

At first Dr. Lution scowled. Then he readjusted his expression and said in an agreeable tone, "Well, hello, David. I'm glad that we've run into each other. I've been wanting to have a word with you about those reports you wrote last grading period."

David swallowed nervously and just nodded. He couldn't help glancing back toward the entrance. He sure wished Billy and the gang would come in.

"Have a seat, David," Dr. Lution said more as a command than an invitation. David sat. Then he stole another hopeful glance behind him and sighed with relief as he saw Billy striding quickly toward them. Dr. Lution also saw Billy and scowled again.

Walking up to Dr. Lution, Billy smiled and put out his hand. Reluctantly, Dr. Lution shook hands with him. "It's nice to meet you, Dr. Lution. I'm Billy James. As you might already know, my friends and I are David's tutors—helping him out on his science reports."

Dr. Lution rolled his eyes at the words *science reports*. "Yes, yes. That's just what I was hoping to talk to David about." By this time, Abel had gotten Darin untied and they were standing behind Billy. "Well," Dr. Lution continued, trying to sound polite, "I guess we'd all better sit down."

Once everyone was seated, Dr. Lution looked straight at David, and said, "David, your previous principal, my daughter, Ms. Lution, found your reports...well...unique and interesting. However, I'm afraid her professional judgment was impaired by unresolved personal trauma, and perhaps by a growing attachment to you and your friends."

Then, in a more stern tone, he continued, "Now, David, I need to make it absolutely clear that I *will not* tolerate mythology, religion, or pseudo-science in *my* classroom." He tapped the booth table hard with his finger to emphasize his words. "If you want to receive good grades in my class, you'll have to *earn* them by using *real* facts to support solid scientific conclusions." Then, Dr. Lution sat back in his seat, folded his arms across his chest confidently, and waited for David's response.

David was quiet for a moment, hoping Billy, or even Darin, would speak up for him. But everyone was quiet. This was his battle, not theirs. So, David cleared his throat and said, "Well, Dr. Lution, sir, I know you've studied a whole lot about evolution for lots of years, but just because creation science doesn't agree with evolution doesn't mean it's not *real* science." Taking a breath, David continued, "Creation scientists are *real* scientists, with *real* Ph.D.'s. They look at the same evidence you look at and use *real* scientific methods to come to truly *scientific* conclusions."

Darin and Abel both nodded their heads vigorously in agreement, but Dr. Lution ignored them. His eyebrows shot down in frustration. Then, pointing a finger at David, he answered, "Young man, your so-called *creation science* is a bunch of bologna!"

David frowned, but answered politely, "Sir, it seems to me that as soon as some evolutionists hear the word *creation*, they cover their ears and close their eyes and say it's not *real* science." Then, leaning back in his booth and crossing his own arms, David concluded, "No offense, sir, but from all the *real* science and *real* evidence I've been reviewing, it seems to me that it's evolution that's a bunch of bologna!"

Dr. Lution tightened his lips and tried to keep his composure. Then, standing up, he looked down his nose at David. "Young man, I plan to speak to your parents about your attitude." Waving an irritated hand toward Billy and the others, he added, "I will also mention my concerns about your spending so much time with these…these…anti-evolution propagandists."

When David showed no signs of backing down, Dr. Lution resorted to pointing his finger again. "I've warned you, David, I will only accept real science, none of that Bible-based nonsense!" Then he turned and walked toward the exit.

"Whew!" Darin let out a long breath. "I guess I'd call *that* a fire-breathing dragon!"

Abel stood up and made a sweeping bow to David. "It is very good to meet you Saint George. Looks like you've fought more than one dragon in your day!"

David was glad for his friends' encouragement, but still felt worried. "Man! I knew Dr. Lution would be tough, but I didn't think he'd be this bad."

Billy looked serious for a moment, but then laughed. "Come on you guys, I mean, if Dr. E. V. Lution, Ph.D. times three, eats at Biggie Burgers, he can't be all bad!"

Then, everyone relaxed some, and Darin called out, "Yabba-dabba-doo—bring on the pterodactyl wings!"

CHAPTER 3

As the jeep traveled along the dark stretch of Lonely Road, Darin and Abel were ready for action. Both were wearing a pair of their *Reality Morphing* sunglasses—set for infrared heat sensing. Both were dressed in black. They looked like a pair of presidential bodyguards. "No way is anyone gonna sneak up on us," Darin bragged.

David tried not to sound nervous as he and Billy discussed the note his mom had found in their mailbox earlier that day. It had been short and pretty simple: "I heard about your disagreement with Dr. Lution at Biggie Burgers. I think I have some information that will help. Meet me on the Lonely Road Bridge at 9:00 p.m. tonight. Park the jeep under the big pine before the bridge. From—*a friend*."

"Well, he sure picked a dark, isolated spot," David said, looking at all the trees that shadowed the small dirt road from the moon's light.

Billy nodded, then told everyone, "Okay, guys, Lonely Bridge is just up ahead. We're supposed to park here under this big pine tree, then go wait for our…um… *friend* on the bridge."

Darin and Abel got out first, scanning all the surrounding trees for warm-blooded life. "Three deer and a raccoon, or maybe an opossum…" Darin reported.

"Four mice, eight voles, two young rabbits, and a prowling bobcat…" Abel added.

"Bobcat?" David repeated in surprise.

"Looks like we got here ahead of whoever we're waiting for," Billy whispered as he and David climbed out of the jeep. Cautiously, they walked over to the bridge that spanned Cherokee Creek. The creek was swollen from the recent rains and made a surprising amount of noise.

"Alert!" Abel whispered. "All three deer and the bobcat are looking up the road. They must hear something coming."

David stepped closer to Billy. And, a few seconds later, a car's bright headlights lit up the narrow dirt road. The vehicle slowed down as it approached the bridge. But the bright headlights kept the group from even being able to see what kind of car it was. Then, suddenly, the car began to pick up speed. Billy and Abel pushed David up against the bridge railing as the car went bouncing past them. Then, as it was driving off the opposite end of the bridge, something was tossed out the driver's window and landed with a thud in the dirt.

After waiting a moment to take in what had just happened, everyone ran toward the small package lying in the road. Darin got there first, but waited for Billy to pick it up.

"Hmmm," Billy said, examining it. "It's a file folder holding different kinds of documents and newspaper articles."

"Anyone get a look at the driver?" Abel asked.

The others shook their heads.

****

That next Wednesday, David was back at the Creation Science Club's Maple Hill workshop. He tossed the thick file folder onto the table for the others to look through. "Man, you guys!" he said excitedly. "Whoever our *friend* is, he sure is fascinated with the idea that man and dinosaurs once existed together! He's got pages and pages of stuff—all sorts of accounts and clues that point to man and dinosaurs living at the same time."

Billy stopped looking through the pages he had picked up to wonder out loud, "Strange that someone would be so secretive about giving us this stuff. I just can't figure out who it might be."

Darin jumped up, waving a page from the pile. "Check it out! This article says that ancient Chinese Emperors used to keep dragons *(or dinosaurs)* as pets."

"Yeah," David said. "There are lots of cool stories. And there are also copies of some authentic historical documents from hundreds, even thousands, of years ago that talk about people seeing dragons or other creatures that sound just like dinosaurs.

Abel held up a paper. "Did you see this? It says here that some cowboys saw a huge leather-winged creature in the desert. Says they even cut a piece of its wing off."

"There's another one in there," David said excitedly, "that talks about two girls, about 120 years ago, who say they rode on the back of a baby dinosaur."

"Okay, okay..." Billy laughed, holding up his hands. "I'm sure that each and every article in here is very...let's say...*interesting*. However, *interesting* doesn't mean *true*. David, for your report, we can only use the articles that have some historical credibility."

Darin looked offended. "Are you suggesting that this story saying a whole town witnessed an alien spaceship come down and take the last five living dinosaurs into outer space might be a hoax?"

David searched through the papers in front of him. "There's a really great article in here about all the ancient legends of dragons from different parts of the world. It talks about how unlikely it would be for so many different countries to come up with such similar *dragons* when they were so isolated from each other."

"Yeah!" Billy agreed. "Already, many scientists are considering that the stories about villages being terrorized by dragons and the legends about knights killing dragons aren't necessarily all mythology. I mean, as that article says, it just seems unlikely that so many different places would have such similar stories. Of course," he continued, "these stories were most likely exaggerated over time—you know, dragons that could talk, and dragons that only accepted young beautiful maidens...stuff like that. Still, the foundation of the legends could be true."

"Here's a good article," Abel said, putting a few pages on the growing *useful paper* pile. "It's about rock and cave drawings in different places that resemble dinosaurs. It says some of the drawings are thousands of years old."

"Super-saawweeeet!" Darin said. "Like, how can anyone ignore Indians and cavemen drawing pictures of dinosaurs? Think about it—dinosaurs were only 'discovered' 200 years ago, and yet, these guys were painting pictures of them thousands of years ago. This is great stuff!"

Billy stopped leafing through the articles to look at David. "Hey, David, just keep in mind that the evolutionists have seen most of these articles, too. They group them together with 'mythology and a bunch of bologna.'"

"Yeah," David answered hesitantly. "I guess I know that all these things aren't proven *facts*. Maybe they're not the same kind of hard evidence as the blood and soft tissues found in the unfossilized dinosaur bones. Still, I think it's important that the possibilities are brought to people's attention—or at least to the attention of Darwin's eighth grade honors science class," he added with a smile.

****

A glint of predatory revenge brightened the raptor's eyes as he slithered from behind one tree trunk to the protection of another. No more than 50 feet away, *the man* was cutting some brush to carry to the farm animals. Another 50 feet farther off was Pudgy, browsing on a broad-leafed bush.

First take down the man—the velociraptor told itself—then the fat little triceratops would be easy prey. Forty feet. The farmer had put down his blade to gather the cut branches. Thirty feet. The farmer bound the fodder. Twenty feet. Of all the perfect luck, the man had actually turned his back to the approaching dragon. With a hissing shriek, the beast rose onto its hind legs and charged toward the farmer. "Yabba-dabba-doo! I guess I'm gonna show you a thing or two!"

As the farmer swung around to face the beast, Billy's voice called from down the hill, "David, your mom's on the phone."

Once again, the velociraptor found itself sprawled at the feet of a 13-year-old boy. "Not again!" Darin complained.

"Don't worry," David said with a laugh. "We'll meet again—you can bet on it." Then, the three friends headed down toward the cabin on Maple Hill.

CHAPTER 4

The Age of the Dinosaurs (Dinosaurs Lived with Man)

by David J. Avila

Introduction

The two most commonly accepted theories concerning *the age of the dinosaurs* involve the very same evidence, but end up with two vastly different conclusions. These different conclusions are really the result of the very different assumptions (foundational beliefs) each theory begins with.

Evolution begins with the assumption (foundational belief) that the earth is billions of years old and that life has evolved very slowly over millions of years. Based on this assumption, evolution has looked at the evidence and come to the conclusion that dinosaurs evolved hundreds of millions of years ago and became extinct about 60 million years ago.

Creation begins with the assumption (foundational belief) that the Bible is true. Based on this assumption, creationists have looked at the evidence and concluded that God created dinosaurs, along with man, on the sixth day of creation, about 6,000 years ago. A true scientist will look closely at both theories (ideas or beliefs) to see which one explains the evidence better.

For this report, I will look at three lines of evidence that show dinosaurs lived thousands of years ago (with man), not millions of years ago. I will use evidence from the Bible, then from history, and finally evidence from a few recent fossil discoveries. In this way, I will show that the evidence makes better sense when we begin with what the Bible makes clear—dinosaurs lived with man.

Dinosaurs in the Bible

The word *dinosaur* was not invented until 1841, so this specific word does not show up in the Bible or in history before that time. However, the Bible and history both tell about real living creatures that fit the description of dinosaurs. First, consider two examples out of the Bible, written less than five thousand years ago—Behemoth and Leviathan.

In Job chapter 40, we're told of a mighty creature that Job must have known about. Behemoth ate grass like an ox. He made his home in the jungle of the reeds and ferns. He had strong and powerful muscles. His bones were as strong as bars of iron. His giant tail swayed like a cedar tree. He was described as chief in the ways of God. No one could capture this creature. Based on this description from the Bible, it sounds like Behemoth was some sort of sauropod, a kind of dinosaur. If Job knew this creature, it couldn't have been extinct *millions* of years ago, but must have lived only a few *thousand* years ago.

In chapter 41 of the book of Job, we find the description of Leviathan, another dinosaur-like creature. He was powerful and graceful. He had a strong neck and breathed smoke and fire out of his nose. His mouth was filled with sharp, fearsome teeth. His back was covered with rows of scales tightly sealed together like armor. Spears and arrows simply bounced right off him. Nothing could make this creature afraid, and he terrified his enemies. This creature fits the description of a dinosaur. It sounds like some of the dragons that have been described around the world.

Dinosaurs in History

Aside from the Bible, we find further historical examples of creatures that match the description of what we know about dinosaurs. The word *dinosaur* couldn't be used to describe them simply because it hadn't been invented yet. Instead, they used words like *large reptile* or *dragon.* These descriptions come from all over the world, and from many different times throughout history. These creatures are described in ancient history books, old science books, artwork, journals, and other historical resources.

An old history book, called *Anglo-Saxon Chronicles,* has accounts of dragons only a thousand years ago. And an old science book, called *Historia Animalium,* claims that dragons were still walking the earth about 500 years ago. These dragons were not legends, but living creatures described in history and science. The descriptions of these dragons match what we know about dinosaurs.

Other written historical accounts include a creature seen in France described as being bigger than an ox and having long, sharp, pointed horns on its head. That could be a triceratops. In Ireland, someone wrote about a large beast with iron nails on its tail. Its head was like a horse's, but it had thick legs and strong claws. It sounds like something from the stegosaurus family. A Greek explorer described a small flying reptile with a snakelike body and bat-like wings.

Similar creatures were also described in Africa and India. Their descriptions point to something like rhamphorhynchus.

Ancient artists from hundreds or thousands of years ago also drew pictures that look like dinosaurs. They didn't recreate dinosaurs from what we know about fossils, like we do today. They were working with real, living models—creatures that walked the earth. For example, an ancient Indian carving discovered at the Grand Canyon looks a lot like an edmontosaurus. There is also an ancient Roman mosaic that shows a long-necked dragon that looks a lot like a tanystropheus.

These examples from the Bible and from written and artistic history show that people knew what dinosaurs looked like long before fossils were discovered and before the word *dinosaur* was even invented. This indicates that dinosaurs must have lived with man.

Recent Fossil Finds

In addition to the historical accounts, there is other strong *physical* evidence that dinosaurs are *not* millions of years old. First, the Liscomb Bone Bed in northern Alaska has thousands of dinosaur bones that appear to be unfossilized. Some even seem to have ligaments still attached to them. This is scientifically possible if these bones are only thousands of years old. But, it would be scientifically questionable to argue that 65 million year old bones actually survived that long unfossilized. However, many evolutionists reject the science behind this issue and cling to their millions of years.

A recent fossil find of a *Tyrannosaurus rex* appears to contain actual red blood cells. The scientists who discovered this found it hard to believe, since "these bones are 65 million years old." So, they performed several tests to prove that these were not actual red blood cells, but all the test results seemed to show that the bone did indeed contain red blood cells. Now, many evolutionists simply reject the evidence that shows blood cells don't last millions of years, in order to hold on to their foundational assumption. They reject scientific evidence for their belief.

Not only have blood cells been found, but also soft, fibrous tissue and complete blood vessels. These fossils were found in temperate regions. One scientist described the tissue as "flexible and resilient." The scientist could even squeeze out the contents of the blood vessels. For tissue like this to survive many millions of years seems to go against operational science. However, if these fossils are simply thousands of years old, then finding blood cells and soft tissue is possible.

Conclusion

The age of the dinosaurs is not something we can observe, test, or repeat. Therefore, the two main theories of the age of the dinosaurs are both historical science, not operational science. They both begin with a *belief* about when dinosaurs existed, and then try to explain the evidence.

Evolution begins with the belief that the earth is billions of years old and that dinosaurs evolved 100's of millions of years ago and became extinct about 60 million years ago. They reject or explain away any evidence that is not compatible with their millions of years. They reject the biblical accounts of animals from thousands of years ago that match the description of dinosaurs. They reject the historical eyewitness accounts of creatures all over the world that match the description of dinosaurs. They won't even accept what the fossils themselves are *saying* by explaining away unfossilized bones, soft tissues, and even surviving red blood cells.

Creation begins with the belief that the Bible is true, and that God created dinosaurs about 6,000 years ago, along with people. Creationists look at all the evidence and see that their theory realistically explains all the evidence.

If you consider both theories carefully, I think you will find that the evidence makes better sense when we begin with what the Bible makes clear—dinosaurs lived with man.

****

Dr. Lution let out a long sigh as he sat down and opened up his laptop to begin an e-mail.

TO: chance@science.qlu.net
FROM: drevlution@science.qlu.net
RE: principalship of DMS

Concerning your recent inquiries, I am glad to inform you that, on the whole, things are going quite well. Although I am tired by the end of each day, being principal and science teacher of DMS is quite fulfilling in its own way. Indeed, it is *rewarding* to know that I am playing a significant role in the molding of the scientists of tomorrow.

I have to smile a bit as I confess that the only challenge I am facing is a boy named David Avila. It was beyond my comprehension that Eva (my daughter and DMS's previous principal) would let a middle school student confuse her solid scientific training. But, I am finding that David is not just a regular student out to maintain a high GPA. He seems to have a much higher goal. It is a delicate situation, as it is a *religious* issue. His father is the pastor of Holy Word Church here in Greenville.

In some ways, David has the makings of a great future scientist—hard working, well researched, and determined. He closely examines the evidence and comes

to well-supported conclusions. It's only his *religious bias* that's holding him back.

Normally, I would steer clear of a battle of *faith vs. fact.* But in this case, David's misconceived notions are starting to influence the other students in the class. In this last report, four other students used *the Bible* as evidence that dinosaurs might have lived with man. I can't let this deception continue. For the sake of the other students, I plan to be firm and factual.

For this reason, I was very happy to see that QLU's new extensive evolution web site is now up and running. It is indeed impressive, worth every penny of the 1.2 million dollars spent on it. I plan to make good use of it in defending and promoting true science with my students.

-Dr. E. V. Lution

PART 2

The Origin of Humans

CHAPTER 5

"*A little more...a little farther!*" Darin Tadue said excitedly to his two puffing friends as they trudged through the fall's first real snow. "I want maximum velocity when I hit that dip right before the drop off. That's the only way I'll break free of the earth's gravitational pull."

"I hope you have a landing plan for when you *re-enter* the earth's gravitational pull," Abel said as he leaned back trying to stretch the giant slingshot a few feet farther. "I mean, they don't call it *Break-neck Canyon* for nothing."

"Like, duh!" Darin responded, readjusting himself on his *Extreme Machine III* snow disk. "Why are you always such a *wet blanket*? Nobody would believe you're *my* twin brother!" This was clearly sarcasm, as the two boys looked exactly alike.

Once comfortable, Darin continued, "Mom sewed me a totally stupendously spectacular parachute." Then he half-smiled and admitted, "Of course, I didn't tell her what I was going to use it for, but," he excused himself, "it's all in the name of science."

David grunted as he slipped in the deep snow. Pulling against the stretchy band with all his strength, he shook his head and said, "Your mom must spend hours a day praying for you. There's no other way you'd still be alive."

"Hey, David-dude, no worries!" Darin said confidently. "I've thought of everything." Then he settled himself deeper into his snow disk. Grabbing the double strength finger-formed comfort grips, he braced his knees against the bubble-rubber kneepads and said, "Commence launch sequence countdown."

Abel and David counted down together. 10…9…at zero, they both fell backwards, simultaneously releasing the slingshot. David shouted, "Remember to pull the ripcord!"

In the split second before he began his race toward *Breakneck Canyon*, Darin whipped his head around. His face was a picture of pure panic. Then, *whoosh*, he was flying. "Oh, nooooooo!" his voice trailed behind him. "I forgot to make a ripcoooo…"

****

Hearing the three short beeps of a jeep's horn outside, David hopped up from the dinner table and gave his mom a peck on the cheek. "Thanks for the burritos!"

Mr. Avila smiled at his son and reminded him, "Make sure Billy knows we're having the Greenville Joint Christmas Service rehearsal at *our* church tomorrow evening."

"And," added Mrs. Avila, "tell Mrs. James that the food committee will be meeting there at the same time."

"Sure thing!" David called over his shoulder as he grabbed his things and ran toward the door.

Once in the jeep, David was uncomfortably quiet. Billy could guess why, and didn't push the issue, but simply started whistling a hymn quietly to himself.

"Isn't that *Out of the Ivory Palaces*? I've always liked that song," David said as he looked out the window at the setting sun.

"Yep!" Billy nodded his head in a thoughtful way. "Seeing what Christ, the King of kings, did for us sure seems to put the ups and downs of our life into perspective."

David glanced at Billy for a second, then looked back out the window. "I guess my mom told you about the grade Dr. Lution gave me on my last report."

Billy sighed. "David, I know it's no fun getting a C. But, we kinda expected it. I mean, when you hit someone where it hurts, they usually hit back." Then he smiled and said in an encouraging tone, "I'd say a C from Dr. E. V. Lution—ultra-evolutionist—is a good sign that you said all the *right* things."

David thought about that for a minute, then smiled. Finally, he even had to laugh. "Yeah, I guess an A from Dr. E. V. Lution would have meant we *didn't* challenge anything about evolution." Then he said in a confidential tone, "Jack and Jill got C's on their reports, too. Jack was mad, but Jill couldn't have cared less. She said she was really writing for her dad, not Dr. Lution, anyway."

****

Up on Maple Hill, Abel heard the jeep pull up and opened the cabin door. Billy and David blew right in, along with a good deal of snow.

"I see why you drive a jeep," David laughed as he stamped the snow out of his boots. Then he lowered his voice and asked Abel, "How's Darin doing?"

Abel and Billy exchanged glances. "He's doing pretty well. He's in the dark room, where it's warmer." Abel motioned toward the back hall. "He's been looking forward to your visit."

David was a little hesitant, but headed back to the cabin's dark room, the smallest of the back rooms. It was a windowless room used for film development and other experiments requiring more heat and less light. David found Darin seated in a big cushiony reclining chair with a portable tray holding snacks on one side, and a table with a laptop and several half made gadgets on the other side. A small TV on the counter was playing an old movie.

Darin sat up excitedly as David entered the room. "Hey, David-dude! It's great to see you! It was getting a little boring around here."

David was still a little uncertain. "Ummm…so, how are things going?"

Darin laughed at David's quiet tone. "Don't be shy! It's just me—*Darin the Diehard*!" he said pointing to the big bandage wrapped around his head. "Complete with a Viking helmet and everything! No little fall into *Break-neck Canyon* is gonna slow down Darin the Diehard—not much anyway."

David pulled up a folding chair and commented, "Billy said you had to have 24 stitches."

"Yeah, yeah," Darin said with a scoff. "That's nothing. Once, when I was a kid, I broke my arm *and* my leg—both at the same time." He paused to think for a moment. "That was the time Abel tried to invent electronic bird wings. We were ten at the time. Then, six months later, he tried again, and I broke my other leg. Boy, was Dad mad. Abel didn't get dessert for a month.

"Anyway, it was around that time that Abel started wimpin' out on me. He gave up on the really exciting inventions to stick with things that don't break any bones." Darin scowled. "I keep telling him, 'it's all worth it in the name of science.' But, he won't agree. But, you agree, don't ya, dude?"

David wasn't so sure about that, so he changed the subject. "Uh…whatcha watchin'?"

"*Planet of the Apes*." Darin answered triumphantly. "Actually, I was just glancing through it. I was really waiting for you to come. I thought it would go great with your next science report—*the evolution of humans*."

David laughed. "*Planet of the Apes*—what a joke!"

****

On the drive back home, David said to Billy, "Looks like Darin the Diehard won't really be up to going to Argentina during Thanksgiving break, huh?"

Billy shook his head with a sigh. " 'Fraid not. I already called my friends and canceled the trip."

"I'm glad," David said. "It wouldn't be the same without Darin."

"That's for sure!" Billy laughed. "Nothing's the same without Darin along."

"Is it because Darin has Asperger Syndrome that he likes to do such dangerous things?"

Billy took a minute to think about that. "No…I think it's more personality based. It's just the AS that gives Darin his all-committed drive to discover new things. You have to realize that when Darin does something dangerous, he honestly *doesn't* think it's very dangerous. Remember, Abel has AS, too, but he's more…uh…*settled* than Darin. I guess he's just taken up the task of watching out for his more adventurous little brother."

"I read an article the other day while I was at the library that said most people with Asperger Syndrome tend to be loners. I thought that was strange since Darin and Abel love being around folks. Is that just because AS affects people in such a different range of ways?"

Billy shook his head. "I think that article might have been a little out of date. Doctors are learning more about AS every day, so only the most recent articles reflect all the new things they're learning."

"So, then, why would the article have said that?"

"Actually, in a way it is true. Many people with Asperger's are loners. However, doctors are now realizing that it's not because they're necessarily genetically inclined to be loners. It seems to be more *learned* than *genetic*.

"You see, most people with AS are not diagnosed as such. So, their differences are usually seen as strange behavior or even bad behavior. They're often misunderstood or shunned by others. They quickly learn to avoid social situations. It's just less stressful for them. However, when they're with people who understand and accept them, they come out of their shell and enjoy social interactions just like anyone else."

"Well, I think Abel and Darin are great!" David said. "Life would be pretty boring without 'em."

Billy nodded, then went back to their original subject concerning the dino-dig in Argentina. "Even though Darin the Die-Hard's accident canceled our original plans, my friends in Argentina know a Bible-believing family that has worked on smaller digs in Argentina for nearly fifteen years. So, I gave the *Soure* family a call, and they said we could come on down anytime Darin was feeling better."

"Hurray!" David whooped. "So, we get to go to Argentina after all! I guess it'll just have to be for my next report."

"Your parents said that you could fly straight from Guatemala—after visiting your grandparents for Christmas—to Argentina, and meet us in San Juan. That'll leave us a full week for dino-digging," Billy explained.

All of the sudden, David leaned toward the windshield. "Look out, Billy! What's that?"

Being careful not to slip on the snowy road, Billy slowed the jeep. Up ahead, in the beam of the headlights, was the figure of a man just visible in the falling snow. He was waving a large red rag and motioning them to the side of the nearly deserted road.

"Look's like someone must have slid off the road and needs some help," Billy said. But, then he added, "Hmmm, I don't see his car."

Once the jeep was stopped, the man didn't wait to talk with Billy. He just started running, signaling for them to follow him. Soon, they were entering the woods close to the road. The man who had stopped them was about 40 feet ahead of Billy and David. It was nearly dark among the trees, and David tripped on a branch under the snow and fell. Billy paused to help him, and called to the man, "Wait! Slow down!"

The man stopped until David was up again. Then, he motioned again and started running. Billy puffed to David, "It seems like he's leading us to Canton Road. It's a small back road through these trees. It wouldn't have been plowed. Maybe his car's stuck there."

"He sure is in a hurry," David panted back. "I hope that doesn't mean someone's hurt."

Billy lifted his cell phone, already in his hand. "If so, we'll call 911."

Soon, David could make out a dark colored SUV through the trees. The engine seemed to still be running and the headlights were on. As they watched, the mysterious man approached the driver's door, opened it, climbed in, and then...shut the door and drove away.

Billy and David stopped and just looked at each other. Then Billy told David to stay where he was, and ran on ahead to Canton Road. After a minute, Billy called, "Hey, come and check this out."

David made his way out of the trees and over to a stump close to where the SUV had been parked. On the stump was the man's red rag. And, under the rag, was a file folder. "Looks like our mystery *friend* has decided to help us again," Billy said, picking up the folder and handing it to David.

CHAPTER 6

"I must say, Mr. James, that it is great luck that you're friends with Dr. Veritas," Dr. Lution said with relief in his voice. "Though I can't imagine that you two have much in common, it has sure been a good break for my honors science class. Who would have guessed that the whole world would be mobbing Dr. Veritas's museum here in small-town Greenville?"

"Well," Billy smiled good-naturedly, "the *Lucy* exhibit is extremely famous. People from all around want to see it."

"Yes," Dr. Lution agreed. "And I'm glad they want to. It is an excellent example of anthropological research. However, I would think the local people—especially students—would get first consideration."

"I guess Teddy has bills to pay just like everybody else," Billy answered.

"Anyway," Dr. Lution continued, without trying to hide his pleasure, "I couldn't have asked for anything better than a private viewing."

During this brief conversation, the students of Darwin's eighth grade honors class—along with all the tutors able to attend—had been excitedly exploring the many small exhibits in the large entrance of Dr. Theodore Veritas's museum.

At nine-thirty exactly, Dr. Ted came out of an *employees only* door to greet his guests. "I want to welcome you all to my Museum of…um…Certain Science." He looked toward David and smiled. Then, looking at Dr. Lution, he said, "Edward, it is good to see you." To the students, he said, "I hope that you will all find your 'visit' with Lucy very… ummm…well, educational and enlightening."

Then, as he took a breath, but was obviously going to continue, a woman's voice came bursting forth. "Allow me, Dr. Lution, sir, to assure you of our unreserved delight in granting you—such a noted scientist—and your students this private showing."

Dr. Ted looked at the professionally dressed, middle-aged woman in order to express his irritation at her interruption.

She, however, met his gaze without flinching and then turned her back on him to address the group in front of her. "My name is Ms. May Dupp. I am the traveling curator of the Lucy exhibit. Now, while you will notice several armed officers hired to guard this exhibit, I am the one who is ultimately responsible for Lucy."

She continued with an air of importance. "I am the only one here considered qualified to provide accurate, up-to-date information and to answer any questions you might have. So, when the time comes, please direct your questions—one at a time—to myself." Then she added almost apologetically, "Of course, however, if Dr. Lution would have anything to add, his comments are very welcome."

David and Darin looked at each other and rolled their eyes. Jack and Jill looked at each other and wrinkled up their noses. Then Abel leaned toward his friends and whispered, "With a name like May Dupp, I'm afraid I might have trouble trusting the authenticity of her answers to my questions." Jill had to swallow her laughter in a choking cough.

Jack whispered, "What's so funny?"

David whispered back, "May Dupp—made-up—don't ya get it?"

Following Ms. Dupp through a maze of tunnel-like false walls, Dr. Lution's class entered a large exhibit room. The room was dimly lit and mysterious music hauntingly filled the room. Along the walls were several large photos of Donald Johanson—the anthropologist who discovered Lucy.

There were also many more photos of other supposed "human ancestor" fossil finds. Each photo had its own dim light above it and a large plaque beside it inscribed with a detailed explanation of the picture and all the pertinent scientific information.

Around the periphery of the room were small, dimly lit glass boxes, each with a small artifact—an ancient human jawbone, a few pieces of a skull, and several bones from a foot.

Then, in the exact center of the room was a glass case about seven feet tall. Several tan-colored spotlights highlighted the fossil remains of a young female australopithecine.

Darin, still wearing a bandage on his head, leaned toward David and whispered, "Kinda feels like they want us to bow down and worship it or something."

David nodded. "It's kinda creepy, huh?"

There was an almost sacred hush in the room as the students took their allotted 20 minutes to read through the information on the walls and to take required notes. No photos were allowed.

Next, Ms. Dupp called the class to gather around the case holding the remains of the australopithecine—nicknamed *Lucy*—long hailed as the "missing link."

Around the fossil remains were ten near-photograph quality paintings of Lucy—an ape-like little *person*. Her arms were a bit too long, but she stood upright and had very human-looking hands and feet. Her face was rather monkey like, but her expression in each picture spoke intelligence and emotion. The artist had carefully made Lucy's eyes looking straight at the viewer; her eyes "spoke" as one *person* to another. In one drawing she was standing by a river. In another she was carrying an armful of fruit. There were even drawings of her sitting with a group of other australopithecines that must have been her family.

Ms. Dupp gave her finely tuned, carefully rehearsed speech concerning what an earth-shattering significance Lucy was to the validation of the evolution of humans.

Finally, she was ready to entertain questions. "I understand that Dr. Lution encouraged you to work together this week to come up with a list of your best questions. I can't think of a better way to prepare for your visit to this extraordinary exhibit." Then she asked, "So, who has the first question?"

Jack quickly raised his hand. When Ms. Dupp pointed to him, he began, "A paleontologist in Switzerland who studied Lucy's ribcage said that he had expected it to be barrel shaped, as in humans, but found it was conical shaped instead, like you see in apes. How do scientists who claim Lucy as an ancestor to humans explain this difference?

Ms. Dupp responded confidently, "Well, that's just what we would expect from a sub-human ancestor—some ape-like qualities, and some human-like qualities."

"Then, how does the evidence reveal the human-like qualities?" Jack continued.

"Well, as I mentioned earlier, because of Lucy's knee joint, Donald Johanson came to the conclusion that she walked upright, as humans now do."

Jack was ready for that one and responded, "But isn't it true that the knee joint that led Mr. Johanson to this conclusion was actually found a year before he discovered the rest of Lucy? We read that it was found more than two miles away and a surprising 200 feet lower in the earth's strata."

May Dupp blinked a few times, then answered, "Well, we have to be careful not to let ourselves get confused by the many *small* details. The overall evidence makes the facts of human evolution quite clear." Then directing her attention away from Jack, she quickly asked, "Does a different student have a question?"

Jill—toward the back of the group—raised her hand. Ms. Dupp smiled and pointed to her. Jill began, "Dr. Brian Richmond identified clear skeletal features that indicate Lucy was a knuckle walker, similar to apes, such as chimpanzees and gorillas. Now, some scientists still hold to the belief that Lucy walked upright and is just carrying some evolutionary leftovers, while others concede that Lucy was actually a hunched over knuckle walker. Which opinion do you hold, and why?"

Ms. Dupp's face fell for a second, then she collected herself and answered quickly, "Well, we all know that a multitude of vestigial features exist in living organisms. From all that I have heard and studied, it is my opinion that Lucy walked upright. However, I don't think knuckle-walkers should be limited to just apes, chimpanzees, and gorillas."

Jill made a puzzled expression and said, "I'm not sure I understand what you mean."

Ms. Dupp answered condescendingly, "I'm sorry. I'm afraid at your scholastic level, you can't expect to understand everything regarding this complex issue."

Dr. Lution frowned. Dr. Veritas tugged his beard and tried to hide his smile.

Another student raised his hand. Ms. Dupp pointed to him, then crossed her arms as if in defense. The boy asked, "According to Richard Leakey, the famous fossil-anthropologist, Lucy's skull is so incomplete that most of it is—quote—*imagination made of plaster of Paris*. Do you agree with this statement, and, if so, has any better fossil evidence been found?"

Ms. Dupp nodded, but kept her arms crossed. "Well, of course, we're continually looking for additional evidence, but remember, these are skilled, trained professionals with years of experience."

The tutor of the boy who had asked the question leaned toward another tutor and whispered, "She didn't even answer his question." The other tutor just shrugged her shoulders.

"Well," the student continued, "from what our class has researched, these 'trained professionals' can't seem to agree on what Lucy is, or what significance she might hold, if any, concerning human evolution. Have any more recent fossil finds shed new light on Lucy?"

May Dupp lifted her chin and tapped her foot before answering. "An exciting array of new australopithecine fossils have been found that do indeed give us a growing understanding of Lucy and others like her."

The boy responded, "That's so cool!" Ms. Dupp smiled and relaxed a bit, until he asked his next question. "So, do these new finds actually support the pictures of Lucy that we see here? I mean, in this showcase, there aren't any hand or foot bones at all. But, in the pictures, the hands and feet look basically human."

Darin and Abel couldn't help giggling at Ms. Dupp's expression. Though Billy shushed them sternly, his amber eyes were twinkling.

"As I said," Ms. Dupp cleared her throat impatiently, "these are trained professionals, skilled in paleontology and anthropology and anatomy. Based on what we know about evolution, these pictures are very accurate."

"Then," the boy asked, "you are saying that the new fossil finds show that Lucy had hands and feet like we do?"

Ms. Dupp ignored the question and pointed to David. "Young man, I thought I saw you raise your hand. Do you have a question?"

"Yes, m'am," David responded politely.

As David began, Dr. Lution's face became stern, and he moved toward the center of the room. Dr. Ted saw the signs of an approaching storm and headed toward the back to stand with Billy and his friends.

David read from his notes, "Dr. Charles Oxnard, Professor of Anatomy and Human Biology, concluded that Lucy and the other australopithecines are more different from both apes and humans than apes and humans are from each other. He seemed to imply that Lucy is unique and is not really qualified to be any sort of sub-human ancestor." Then, looking up, he asked, "In your opinion, how is this relevant to the theory of human evolution?"

May Dupp's voice was obviously strained as she answered. "Well, Lucy is certainly unique. That's part of what makes her so relevant to the theory of human evolution. Each unique transitional form leads to the next evolutionary step in…in…evolution."

"That is the *end* of this question and answer session!" Dr. Lution spoke out with authority.

"But, sir…Dr. Lution…" several voices spoke up. "We have more questions…"

Dr. Lution pointed to the exit and repeated, "That is the *end* of this question and answer session. I will join you momentarily out by the museum's main entrance!"

As the class filed respectfully out of the exhibit room, Dr. Lution turned to May Dupp. "Ms. Dupp! In the future, I hope that you will be better prepared to answer the questions of *eighth grade* students!"

"Sir," Ms. Dupp answered defensively, "I have never before had a problem answering *anyone's* questions. It is obvious that someone has given them all the *wrong* questions to ask."

"Obviously!" Dr. Lution agreed. "However, that does *not* excuse your taking the liberty to fabricate plausible-sounding answers that have no factual foundation. Science is supposed to be *fact*-based."

"Well, then, Dr. Lution—Mr. Ph.D. times three—" she answered through tight lips, "the *fact* is that I didn't hear *you* offering any answers of any kind!" And she stomped out of the room.

****

Out in the museum entrance hall, Dr. Veritas was explaining some of the exhibits to the waiting students and tutors. Dr. Lution came in like a storm. "I want to know right now who gave my students those questions to ask Ms. Dupp!" He looked accusingly at Billy.

Billy shook his head, "Don't look at me." But he couldn't help chuckling.

"I don't believe you!" Dr. Lution nearly shouted. "Of all the unprofessional setups...and, you call yourself a *scientist...*"

Then David interrupted. "Excuse me, Dr. Lution, sir. But, honestly, Mr. James had nothing to do with it. I'm the one who had all the information."

Dr. Lution turned to David. "So, I'm supposed to believe that *you*, a 13-year-old middle school student, came up with those questions all by yourself? I am not a *fool*!"

Jack spoke up. "Dr. Lution, it wasn't just David. The whole class looked through the information David had. And we thought, 'Hey, if we've got these questions, then the people in charge of the Lucy exhibit will be the best ones to answer them.'"

Dr. Lution responded sternly, "You *knew* they were exactly the kind of questions no one can answer with any confidence!"

Jill asked, "Then why did Ms. May Dupp answer them so confidently? Were her answers all made up? Was she just *professionally lying*?"

"Oh, I get it," Jack whispered to himself. "May Dupp. Made up."

Dr. Lution decided not to answer Jill's question. Instead, he turned back to David and asked in a no nonsense tone, "So, who gave you all this *information* you so eagerly shared with your classmates?"

David tried not to be intimidated. "A *friend* of mine. And it wasn't Billy or Darin or Abel. Like I said, they haven't even looked at the information I have."

Dr. Lution took a step closer to David, "Who *is* this *friend* of yours?"

David opened his mouth to explain, but Dr. Veritas interrupted, "Edward, I'm sorry, but your class's time is up. If you'll notice, a line is forming outside the museum. I'll have to ask you to leave now. Have a good day."

CHAPTER 7

Later that week, David and the gang were all in Billy's jeep heading toward Maple Hill. Darin was trying his best to convince David to help him re-test his parachute—ripcord now included.

"Better wait till your doctor says you're fit to try it yourself, Darin. I value my life too much. Anyway, I have to live long enough to convince Dr. Lution that people didn't evolve from some kind of ape-like ancestors."

"What do you mean?" Abel asked innocently. Then, in a Ms. May Dupp-like voice, he quoted, "The overwhelming evidence makes the facts of human evolution quite clear."

"As clear as mud-water," Darin smirked as they pulled off Pioneer Road and drove up toward Maple Hill Cabin.

"Say, Billy," David asked, "why is it that you and the T-twins hang out here, instead of at your house off of Millersport Road?"

Darin answered for Billy. "Well, this here cabin used to belong to Mrs. James' grandparents. They left it to Mrs. Carmen and Billy in their will, but since Billy already had that nice place off of Millersport, they decided to make this his office and workshop."

"Besides," Abel spoke up, "every club has to have a clubhouse. We can't meet at Billy's cause Mrs. Carmen is always teaching little girls how to play the piano or how to sew and cook."

Billy turned to David as he put the jeep into park. "The truth is, Carmen evicted us after Darin put a walking stick insect on Little Lucy Standard's head."

"While she was making muffins," Abel added.

"She called me a *geek*," Darin accused.

"She poured the whole cup of flour she was holding right onto her own head trying to get that bug off…" Abel started to laugh.

"I know I'm a geek. I'm glad I'm a geek. But, Little Lucy said it to be *mean*," Darin explained to David. "Don't you think she should have had better manners?"

David smiled. "My mama would say that *you* should have turned the other cheek, not put a big ol' bug on her head."

Darin shrugged. "It's just what I happened to be holding at the time."

"Man, the flour kept flying and the milk was knocked over and six eggs were smashed on the floor before Mrs. Carmen finally got that bug out of Little Lucy's hair…" Abel wheezed, he was laughing so hard.

****

In the cabin, David pulled out a stack of papers and put them on the table for the others to see. "You're not gonna believe all the stuff in here. Whoever our *friend* is, he sure has a lot of doubts about people evolving from apes." He picked up a third of the pile and said, "All these pages, 130 in all, are articles that disprove all the celebrated pre-human fossil finds. Some of them were mistakes, some presupposed conclusions, some outright frauds."

Billy picked up the next bound section from the pile. "Hmmm...this one's titled, *Articles by prominent evolutionists that admit the evidence doesn't point to human evolution*. Wow, that could be embarrassing for the *big people* in evolution."

"But, look," David pointed out, "right in that pile are quotes straight from several of those big people in evolution—I mean the *top* big people—who actually admit outright that evolution is really just a *belief*. Some even come right out and say that, against the evidence, they *choose* to believe evolution rather than having to believe in a creator."

"What's this last pile?" Darin asked as he grabbed it up. "Says here, *The purposeful use of artistic license to persuade the public to believe in evolution in spite of the lack of evidence*."

David explained, "That pile is full of pictures of all kinds of art work—drawings, paintings, statues, museum showcases, video clips—all kinds of examples of *artistic interpretations* of all the different *great fossil finds*. There's one example in there of this picture of the *Nebraska man*. I mean, it's an ape-ish looking man standing there picking an apple from a tree. But, the whole ape-man, and the whole idea of what he looked like, came from a tooth—one single tooth. They drew a whole ape-man from *one single tooth*."

Billy added, "Think about it. Kids read this stuff in a science book. They're told it's true. They don't really understand it, but they see this picture of an ape-man that likes to eat apples. What sticks in their mind? This—*There was once an ape-man. People must have evolved from apes*."

David jumped back in. "And to clinch it, that one single tooth that they used to create the entire Nebraska Man turned out to be a pig's tooth. *Yep*, a *pig*'s tooth." He laughed, then sighed. "That part," he added, "is also in the first stack—in the *mistake* section."

Darin shook his head in disbelief. "That was one *big* mistake."

Then Abel came into the room with two large bowls of popcorn and four big mugs of warm spiced cider on a tray. "Well," he smiled, "this stuff sounds just like the kind of *facts* Dr. Lution is looking for."

They all laughed. Then Darin reached up to hold his healing head. "I think *these facts* are going to give Dr. E. V. Lution—Ph.D. times three—one very factual *headache*!"

****

At the top of the banks of *Purgatory Plunge*, Billy reassured David, "Don't worry, you can't die. There's nothing to run up against. Eventually, it just levels out and you stop. It's completely safe."

"If it's so safe," David asked, settling himself into Darin's *Extreme Machine III* snow disk, "why aren't you sitting in this thing, letting *me* reassure *you*?"

"Ummm...I guess you've got me there!" Billy laughed.

Darin came huffing up the hill toward David. "Okay, dude, just remember, when you reach near maximum speed, Abel will wave the red flag. That's when you need to pull the ripcord. Then we can see how well my parachute really works."

David's face began to register some serious doubt. "I'm not so sure..."

But Darin didn't give David a chance to finish. Instead, he pushed the disk over the bank, and yelled, "Don't worry, David-dude, it's all in the name of science!"

David's voice streamed back behind him, "That's what I was afraid of..."

CHAPTER 8

The Origin of Humans
(The World's First Man)

by David J. Avila

Introduction

The latest scientific ideas concerning the origin of mankind show that there are *two* very different theories. Both evolutionists and creationists have the same *evidence* to examine. However, they arrive at completely different *conclusions*. Their vastly different conclusions actually come from their vastly different starting assumptions.

Evolution *begins* with the assumption that evolution is true. It says that the evolutionary tree begins with a single cell branching out into all kinds of life, with man and apes branching off from a common ancestor. Evolutionists begin with this belief and then search the physical evidence for *missing links*.

Creationists *begin* with the assumption that the Bible is true. So we have the complete picture—all the animals were created after their kind, and God created the first man, Adam, in his own image. Therefore, we did not evolve from single-celled organisms, and there are no missing links. People do differ in size, shape, and color, but the physical evidence shows that people have always been people.

For this report, I will first look at one of evolution's *best* "transitional forms." Then I will look at some of the claimed missing links leading to the "evolution of humans." Finally, I will show that the evidence makes better sense when we begin with what the Bible says, that God created Adam—the world's first man.

Whale Evolution

A *transitional form* is a *missing link* that's been found. Up-to-date science textbooks and evolution web sites offer the transitional forms from land mammal to whale as one of their *most excellent examples*. They have wonderful pictures of a land mammal evolving into a webbed swimmer, then into a swimmer with shrinking legs, then into a whale. But, what does the actual fossil evidence show?

The QLU (Quantum Leap University) evolution web site shows *Pakicetus* looking half land mammal, half webbed swimmer—a *perfect* transitional form between land mammal and whale. But the actual fossil evidence only includes some fragments of the skull and lower jaw—that's it—no leg bones, no arm bones, no backbone—*nothing!* From this (almost nothing), an artist who believes in evolution created this transitional form. Honestly, if I offered this kind of evidence in one of my science reports, the whole school would hear the teachers laughing about it in the teachers' lounge. Later, when a more complete *Pakicetus* skeleton *was* found, it turned out to be a regular land runner, and didn't look anything like evolution's imagined transitional form.

Next, in the official Darwin Middle School science textbook, we find *Ambulocetus* swimming around chasing fish. Though more fossil evidence was found than with pakicetus, the important parts of the skeleton are still missing. But again, the artist gladly filled in the missing pieces to create the perfect image of a transitional form. The textbook also fails to mention that *Ambulocetus* is really *ten times smaller* than the next evolutionary step—*Basilosaurus*. These two evolutionary steps are shown by the artist to be about the same size—making it seem more feasible. My teacher would probably call that *fudging the data.*

These transitional forms (missing links) seem to be the best proof evolution has to offer. Although their *made-up pictures* wonderfully support the belief that whales evolved from land mammals, the actual fossil evidence doesn't support this at all.

Human Evolution

The evidence of transitional forms (missing links) in "human evolution" is similar to the evidence for whale evolution. Because evolutionists are determined that evolution is true, any evidence they find (no matter how miniscule) is interpreted as an important missing link. Then, they turn to artists to help them convince the general public that human evolution is a fact. Let's consider a few examples.

In 1912, an amateur fossil hunter discovered the skull (and nothing more) of what became known as *Piltdown Man.* Several drawings of the entire Piltdown Man—head, body, arms, and feet—were widely publicized. It seemed to be the genuine sub-human ancestor of man. It wasn't until 50 years later that Piltdown Man was shown to be a fraud—an ape's jaw attached to a human skull.

In 1922 a single tooth (only one, nothing more) was found. From this single tooth, anthropological experts determined that it was the tooth of a pre-human transitional form. Artists soon had both drawings and statues of the entire *Nebraska Man*. Yes, he looked exactly like a pre-human transitional form should look. A few years later, however, it was determined that the tooth was actually from a pig. Oops!

Next we have the *Neanderthals*—the sub-humans with heavy eyebrows who walked hunched over. Finally, here was a nearly complete skeleton—irrefutable proof. The most famous scientific periodicals and magazines eagerly printed hundreds of artistic interpretations of Neanderthals. Museums proudly displayed models of this missing link in human evolution. It was later discovered, however, that Neanderthal Man was more likely an arthritic old man who suffered from a disease that deformed his bones. Neanderthal skeletons found today seem to show that Neanderthals were as human as we are—*not* a missing link.

Then *Ramaphithecus* was discovered. Based only on a jawbone and a few teeth, scientists "knew" that this sub-human ancestor walked upright. Later discoveries, however, showed that Ramaphithecus was actually an orangutan. Another scientist was excited by the discovery of a skullcap—*Orce Man*, but he turned out to be nothing more than a young donkey (Orce Man, not the scientist).

Lucy—The Missing Link

Perhaps the most famous *missing link* in human evolution ever discovered is *Lucy*. The evidence is the fossilized skeleton of an australopithecine that is about 40% intact. The jaws, teeth, face, and brain-case are all similar to that of an ape. But Don Johanson, who discovered Lucy, claimed that she walked upright. "I found a human-like knee joint that proved beyond doubt that our ancestors walked erect." However, he avoided mentioning that this *key* knee joint was found more than two miles (yes, *miles*) away, and 200 feet lower in the strata than the rest of the Lucy skeleton. Later research seems to go against Johanson's claim that Lucy walked upright—she was found to have had wrists like knuckle walkers, such as chimpanzees and gorillas.

Beyond Physical

Being human is more than walking upright. In fact, being human goes far beyond our physical body. What is inside a person is what really makes him or her human. Psychologists study it. We often talk about it. But it's completely intangible. It can't be counted or measured or photographed. Yet, what is inside—making us truly human—is 100% real.

If life is nothing more than evolution's *survival of the fittest*, why would anyone even think of giving up his or her life for another, even a stranger? But people do. Why would anyone sacrifice or even endanger themselves in the pursuit of knowledge? Again, people do. Why would one man choose to *cleave* himself to only one woman, severely limiting his offspring producing abilities? How can it be that people with great beauty, health, wealth, and fame, might not have peace or joy? How can it be that people trapped in a life of poverty and suffering can have joy unspeakable and peace beyond measure? It's because these things come from the inside. They come from the *soul* of the person.

The Bible tells us that we are created in the image of God. He gave us our soul. Like God, who designed the universe and this human body, I have a mind. I can think, understand, and create. Like God, who was brokenhearted with the sin of mankind, I have emotions. I can be happy or sad, angry or excited. Like God, who chose to give His only Son for our sins, I can choose to do good, or I can choose evil. To be human is far more than evolution or science can explain. Birth is too amazing. Death is too tragic. Eternity is truly in our hearts. And love goes far beyond survival of the fittest.

Conclusion

The two theories on the origin of mankind are as different as can be. Evolution begins with the belief that all of life has evolved by chance over billions of years. Therefore, human beings are nothing more than the result of millions of years of random mutations and natural selection. Evolutionists look at the fossil evidence and try to make it fit into this belief. Regardless of what the evidence (or lack of evidence) shows, they stick to this belief.

Creation, on the other hand, begins with the belief that the Bible is true, that God created people as people. This makes better sense of the fossil evidence, because it says we should not find any missing links or transitional forms—and we don't. Creation also gives us a clear understanding of what it means to be truly human, and tells us why being human goes beyond the physical and into the intangible. It is because we are created in God's image, just like Adam—the world's first man.

* * * * * * *

Dr. Edward Lution swallowed down two aspirin with what was left in his coffee cup. Then, rubbing his forehead, he turned his attention to his computer.

TO: chance@science.qlu.net
FROM: drevlution@science.qlu.net
RE: principalship of DMS

Oh my! I don't know that I've ever been so tired since preparing for my last oral exams. This week has been just unbelievable. Discipline is not a problem at DMS. Most of the students—even the *rebels without a cause*—respect me (or fear me) enough to stay in line. Actually, it's the *good* students that have given me this headache!

Honors Science Class. I wish my daughter had never started the blasted thing!

Fairy tales, mythology, legends...I can defend evolution against such nonsense. But, tell me, how can I defend evolution against itself—or maybe its *lack* of self. For this last report, nearly half the kids in my class had a heyday with any and every misconception, mistake, and outright lie that has ever plagued the research of the evolution of humans.

I can only blame myself. Why did I ever think *the evolution of humans* would make a good report topic? We just haven't had enough time to find all the supporting evidence we need to really back up what we already know to be true.

David Avila, the ringleader of this uprising, is an interesting young man. He definitely has the makings of a future leader. I'm hoping that I can convince him of his misconceptions. But it's a bit sticky, since his parents are encouraging his anti-evolutionary views. (As I mentioned before, his father is a minister.) However, in his report, he did bring up an interesting point about humans being much more than physical beings—that we go beyond the tangible.

Well, one thing I'll say for David is that he's a bold young cuss. You should have read his report! Then today, after school, I found an envelope on my desk. Believe it or not, it was an invitation to a special joint Christmas service being held by several of the Greenville churches.

I highly doubt he expects me to come. But, I've been thinking about what my daughter, Eva, once said to me—

something about "how can we defend evolution against religion if we don't look at the foundation of why they believe what they believe." I guess David's Christmas service will be the start of my latest research.

-Ed Lution

****

Sitting at the back of the church, Dr. Lution considered all that he was taking in. David's father had not preached the expected *Mary Rides the Donkey* sermon. Instead, he had spoken about different passages from the Old Testament book of Isaiah. Even when the sermon was over, and a bunch of giggling kids ran onto the stage, Edward could still hear Pastor Avila boldly declaring, "People walking in darkness have seen a great light..." Different words from the sermon echoed in his mind: "Immanuel, God with us...Surely this is our God...Here is your God."

Up on the church's stage, Dr. Lution noticed David and several other kids he recognized from school dressed up like shepherds. While the children sang about the angels' announcement to the shepherds, Billy James, dressed as an angel, complete with halo, was being chased by a real live flock of lambs that had decided he looked the most like their mama. Everyone was laughing and cheering. But Dr. Lution's eyes kept going back to his borrowed Bible, back to what was written in the book of Isaiah.

For the evening's finale, the choir led the congregation in singing everyone's favorite Christmas songs. Edward looked up and noticed a woman across the aisle from him. Her smile reminded him of his own dear Marie. He realized he hadn't been in a church since her funeral. How she would have laughed at his hiding in the back of the church.

Suddenly, almost against his will, Marie's face was before him. He could see her standing under the mistletoe she always insisted on hanging up. He could feel her hand reaching up to touch his face as she wished him, "A very merry Christmas!" as she had always done, even the year she died. Realizing that the tears were streaming down his face, Dr. Lution stood up and quickly escaped out into the cold night air.

Late that night, Edward Victor Lution sat alone by his fireplace. For the first time in over 20 years, he let the memories come and go as they pleased. Smiles and tears mixed together as he let his heart remember the sweetest years of his life—the years he had shared with Marie. As he dreamed away, he forgot about the tangible—facts, proof, evidence. For tonight, at least, the intangible was quite as real as the tangible.

PART 3

Fossil Formation

CHAPTER 9

Dr. E. V. Lution looked curiously at the dark sunglasses on his desk. All the students in his honors science class had already put theirs on. And all the hoots and hollers, and giggles and acting out you would expect from a group of excited middle school students (it was only two days before the start of Christmas break) was now taking place.

Looking out at his students' good-natured pranks, Dr. Lution paused to consider—six weeks ago he would have been disgusted with their conduct. A month ago he would have been angered by it. But today, it was an effort to repress his own rising anticipation as he donned the glasses David Avila had given him.

"Okay, class. Time to calm down. Everyone back to their seats," Dr. Lution said from behind his dark glasses. Then he turned to David. "You may begin your presentation."

David put on his own *R.M.* (*Reality Morphing*) glasses. Then, licking his lips a bit nervously, he began. "For my presentation, I chose to do *How the Bible Presents Noah's Flood.*" Dr. Lution's eyebrows drew down, but he didn't say anything. David continued, "Now, since I only have 15 minutes, I decided to make the first part of the presentation a ten minute clip. Then, the last few minutes will be given to a question-answer session."

David sat down in Dr. Lution's swivel chair at the front of the room. Then, seeming to talk to no one in particular, David said, "Begin pre-recorded clip on *How the Bible presents Noah's Flood.*"

A computerized female voice responded through the earpieces of everyone's glasses. "Processing...Now playing *How the Bible Presents Noah's Flood.*" The students all giggled and touched the sides of their glasses. Dr. Lution nodded, clearly impressed.

Before everyone's eyes appeared a scene. An old, bearded man was high on a rock speaking to the gathered crowds. "Turn away from doing wrong. Do what's right or judgment is sure to come." The people scoffed and laughed at him.

Then, David started to narrate. "In the days of Noah, people had become more and more wicked. They were so evil that God was sorry He had made mankind." Scenes of violence and hatred, idolatry, and greed filled the screen. "Only one man found favor with God—Noah." Everyone could see the graying man praying on his knees to God.

David continued, "When God could no longer hold back His judgment, He spoke to Noah, telling him He was going to destroy the earth with a massive, global Flood. He told Noah to build an ark that would save Noah's family, and two of every kind of land dwelling creature and seven of some certain kinds. God gave Noah very specific directions on how to build this giant boat." The students' glasses showed Noah and his sons building a humongous rectangular ship. As the building progressed, a timeline at the bottom of the screen showed 100 years passing.

Some of the students oohed, and one boy commented, "Man, that thing's *huge!*"

In the next scene, animals began to enter the ark: lions, bears, rabbits, kangaroos, and bats; snakes, turtles, and lizards; doves, hawks, cardinals and cranes. Then, a gasp arose from the students. Other animals were beginning to enter the ark—dinosaurs: pteranodons, apatosaurs, stegosaurs, and even a young pair of tyrannosaurs.

David responded to his classmates' surprise. "If we follow the Genesis record, dinosaurs where created at the same time as man—on the sixth day of creation. Therefore, dinosaurs would have been included among the animals Noah cared for on the ark. The Bible says *all* land animals."

The scene changed. The door of the ark was shut. A hurricane-like storm began beating on the ark. Sheets and sheets of rain poured down. The scene panned out to show volcanoes beginning to erupt, giant earthquakes splitting the earth, and water rushing up out of the ground.

David spoke as the scenes played. "Noah's Flood wasn't just a 40-day rain shower. The Bible tells us that, not only were the heavens opened, but also that *the springs of the great deep burst forth*. Water wasn't the only issue in Noah's Flood. Massive destruction and reformation was taking place all over the earth." The students could all see huge land masses splitting apart and smashing together to form new mountains under the raging waters.

"All land dwelling life was destroyed, except for the people and animals on the ark." A volcanic eruption blanketed an entire colony of nesting dinosaurs. Tidal waves came crashing down on fleeing people and animals. Fish and sea creatures tried to flee the boiling waters spewing up from the ocean vents—some survived, many did not. Blankets of mud-filled waters buried whole herds of fleeing animals. Ash, dirt, mud, and sand filled the rising waters, overtaking and burying everything in its path.

Everyone in the room was quiet. Dr. Lution found himself grasping the sides of his desk. This was intense!

David spoke again. "After 40 days and 40 nights, the rains stopped. The Bible says that as the waters steadily receded from the earth, the ark came to rest on the mountains of Ararat. God sent a wind to dry up the earth more quickly. Still, Noah and the animals had to remain in the ark for many months before God told them that they could leave."

Dr. Lution and the students watched the waters going down around the world. Mountains appeared first. Then, grass and plants began to grow. Noah's family removed the ark's roof, and hundreds of winged beasts flew to freedom. The non-flying animals mooed and hissed and trumpeted and pawed in anticipation. Finally, the door was opened for the animals to escape their confinement. It was an amazingly jubilant commotion.

"After leaving the ark," David summarized, "Noah and his family built an altar of thanks to God for saving them. At this time, God promised to never again send a worldwide Flood. As a reminder of his promise, God painted a rainbow across the sky." Scenes of beautiful and magnificent rainbows from many well-known regions around the world filled everyone's glasses.

As the rainbows continued to shine before the students, David asked, "Now…does anyone have any questions?"

A boy in the back commented, "How do you know that's what the ark looked like? I mean, all the pictures I've ever seen were just kind of a regular little boat with a bunch of animals scrunched into it." Several students giggled.

Almost before the boy finished, the computerized voice responded. "Noah's ark was 450 feet long, 75 feet wide, and 45 feet tall, with a volume of 1.5 *million* cubic feet." The voice intoned, "The measurements are found in Genesis chapter 6."

David interjected, "We often see the cute pictures of a boat that could hardly hold a dozen animals. But, they're just that—cute pictures. The real ark was as long as 1 1/2 football fields, as tall as a five story building, and had more cargo space than 500 railroad cars."

"Way cool!" the boy responded.

Jill spoke up. "Uh, my uncle says that there's no way even a huge ark could hold two of every kind of animal. What about that?"

"Processing..." While the glasses loaded information, wild cats began to cross the screen—a tiger, a lion, a saber tooth cat, and an ocelot. "It is often erroneously summarized that every type of animal known today had to be on the ark. It is likely that God brought only representatives of each animal *kind* to Noah, for example, the equine (horse-like) kind, the canine (dog-like) kind, the cattle kind, and so on. This would make the *maximum* number of animals on the ark around 15,000."

Next, as an *Allosaurus*, a *T. rex*, and a *Carcharodontosaurus* roared into the students' faces. The computerized voice continued, "A train with the same cargo space as Noah's ark would hold over 100,000 sheep. Only about 10% of the animals would have been larger than a sheep. So the ark could easily hold 15,000 animals and enough food to feed them for over a year."

Dr. Lution tapped his chin with his finger, deep in thought. A girl in the front row started to ask a question, but Dr. Lution interrupted. "So, according to this clip, the Bible says that Noah's Flood was *more* than a flood?"

"Affirmative," the glasses answered.

"Creation scientists believe that mountains were built and ocean trenches were formed during the Flood?"

"Affirmative," the glasses agreed.

"And that, perhaps, it was even at this time that the continents were divided from one land mass into the several we know today?"

"Possible," the voice answered, "but not fully confirmable."

"Ahhh..." Dr. Lution went back into his own thoughts.

The girl in the front row spoke up again, "So, what about all that water and mud all over the place in that little movie. I mean, all kinds of animals and even fish and whales were, like, buried alive. Could that be why there are so many big groups of animals fossilized together?"

"Ahhh...hmmm..." Dr. Lution nodded his head waiting for his glasses to answer the girl's question. Everyone noticed that David's presentation time was over, but quietly ignored this fact and finished out the rest of the class by asking good questions and getting good, solid, scientific answers.

CHAPTER 10

David stepped out of the concourse and into the airport terminal. The place was packed with Argentines returning home after Christmas visits abroad. Suddenly, from above the crowd, a flashing neon sign appeared. It simply said, *David-dude*. David laughed and began pushing his way through the crowd toward the sign.

"Yo! David-dude!" Darin swatted David on the arm. "How was Christmas in Guatemala?"

"Great!" David answered. "I can't believe my dad's whole family was crammed into my grandparents' little house." Rubbing his stomach, he added, "I think I gained ten pounds."

Billy laughed and grabbed up David's carry-on bag. "Let's get out of here. We can talk in the taxi. We'll be spending the night here in San Juan, then head out to the Soures' dig site first thing in the morning."

"Where's Mrs. Carmen? I thought she said she'd come on this adventure with us."

"Aw," Darin laughed. "She wimped out on us."

"No way!" Abel explained. "A widowed friend of hers had an emergency appendectomy, so Mrs. Carmen decided to stay and help her out for a few days."

"Gimme a break!" Darin joked. "That's all just an excuse—she wimped out."

Billy stopped in mid-stride and looked Darin in the eye. "Should I tell Carmen you said that?"

Darin's face went pale and he put a hand up to his cheek. "Oh, no, Billy, please don't tell her. Please. I won't tease any more."

David leaned toward Abel. "Why's Darin so scared of Mrs. Carmen?"

Abel laughed. "Mrs. Carmen's a strong lady, but she's as sweet as dutch apple pie. Darin's not scared of her. He's just scared that if he offends her, she might not make him any more of her famous cookies."

****

That evening, the Creation Science Club was settled in their low-rate, but quaint, hotel suite. It was set up like a rectangle. It had two very small bedrooms, a visiting area, and a bathroom. These rooms were set around a small open porch right in the center of their rooms. Billy smiled and explained that it was *natural air-conditioning*. Darin frowned and called it *an open invitation to mosquitoes*.

While Billy and David were out investigating dinner options, Darin and Abel flipped on the small TV in the corner of the visiting area. But, after a couple of minutes, Darin cocked his head to the side and asked Abel, "Hey, what's that buzzing sound?"

Abel listened, then said in a mischievous tone, "Sounds like a giant Darin-eating mosquito to me."

"Ha, ha." Darin made a sour face. "That's so funny I forgot to laugh." But, he swatted the air around him just to be safe. Then he got up to investigate. In a minute he had stopped in front of David's backpack. "Sounds like it's coming from David-dude's pack."

Abel shrugged. "Maybe it's his cell phone."

"Naw," Darin said. "He didn't bring one. Remember, we decided only Billy would carry a phone. The rest of us are going to use our *Muf-ToW* bands (that's *multi-functional telecom wrist bands*) to stay connected."

The pack kept buzzing, and Abel and Darin kept staring at it until they heard Billy turning the key in their suite door. Then, Billy and David walked over to the backpack and they all spent a moment staring at it together. Finally, Billy reached down and unzipped one of the front pockets, then carefully reached in. He pulled out a couple of small note pads, a few pens and several pencils. Then, he lifted up a six inch long black cylinder. The end of it had a flashing red light, and it emitted a clear buzzing sound.

"I don't have a clue what *that* is," David said with a note of curiosity in his voice. "I've never seen it before."

Billy inspected it closely and exclaimed, "Look, here! On the side it says in silver letters, *Open—a friend.*"

David, Abel, and Darin all gathered close to Billy. "Totally, like, bizarro!" Darin said. "I can't believe our *friend* actually found us in Argentina."

Billy handed the cylinder to David. "You'd better figure out how to get it to stop buzzing and flashing. Then, we'll do like it says, and open it."

But Darin snatched it and held it between folded hands. "Aw, David-dude, let me do it," he begged. "Please—huh! Please! You know this is what I live for...please!"

David sat down at the table in the open center of the suite. "Okay, Darin. Go for it."

Darin spent several minutes inspecting and explaining the intricacies of the little device. "Really quite ingenious.

See, it has a tiny little timer here—our *friend* must have preset it to start buzzing *after* we had arrived in Argentina."

Billy nodded. "Yeah, he could have put it in your backpack any time in the last couple of weeks."

Darin started to explain where he guessed their friend had gotten the parts to build his contraption. But David said, "Come on, just open it."

So, Darin carefully unscrewed the lid. Then, he turned the cylinder upside down. Everyone held their breath, unsure of what to expect. Out slid a neatly folded and rolled piece of paper. David unfolded it carefully and smoothed it out on the table for all to see. It was a two-sided map. One side was a general map of a pretty large area. The other was a detailed close-up showing certain landmarks and geologic features.

Billy leaned forward. "Hmmm...here's San Juan, right where we are now. And, here's northern Ischigualasto, that's where we're headed. Look here, there's a star just to the southwest of Red Ridge."

"Whoa, check this out!" Abel pointed after David had turned the map to the more detailed side. "It says, *The Fossil They Never Wanted Us to Find*."

Everyone looked at each other. Then Billy said, "Looks like our *friend* has set us up for a real treasure hunt!"

****

Sitting under the tent at the Soures' excavation camp, everyone sipped from their glasses of lemonade (no ice), while Mr. Terry Soure introduced his family. "This is my wife Julia. But, ever since we got engaged, I've called her *Dinah*. So, she's been *Dinah* ever since."

Billy smiled. "Well, I guess it only makes sense. If you're a *pterosaur*, then you should marry a *dinosaur*."

"Exactly!" Terry laughed. "But Dinah put on the breaks when it came to naming our children." Pointing to his son who was walking up to the tent, Terry said, "This is Steve—but, he chose the nickname *Stego*—as in Stegosaurus."

Steve, a.k.a. Stego, pointed to a pretty girl coming out of a small private tent. "That's my sister, Bekah. But we all call her Baryonyx—the *heavy claw*."

"We do not!" Dinah laughed. "We just call her Bekah or Rebekah. Though," she added with a mischievous smile, "when she was little, she did like us to call her *Tulip-Daisy* after her two favorite flowers."

"Mommmmm!" Bekah rolled her big brown eyes as she took a seat by the table. "You guys must be the team Jim Young told us about." She smiled at Darin. "Glad you came. It'll be fun to work with someone different for a while."

Terry stood up and motioned for the others to follow him. "We'll show you all around the camp."

David and Abel stood up, but Darin just sat there—frozen. He hadn't moved since Bekah had smiled at him. David said his name twice, but he still didn't move. Abel waved his hand in front of his eyes, but Darin didn't even blink.

David and Abel looked at each, then said in unison, "Oh, no! He's twitterpated!"

David tried giving Darin a shove, but it only caused a lovesick sigh to escape from his lips. So, as his brother, Abel knew what had to be done. Picking up a bottle of water, he emptied it on Darin's head.

Sputtering and spluttering, Darin jumped up and shook the water off his head, but he didn't try to retaliate. Instead, he looked all around and asked, "Hey, where'd she go?"

Abel and David shook their heads and said, "Pitiful, just pitiful." Then they took him by the arms and led him in the direction Billy and the others had gone.

Terry brought them to a large, low-riding vehicle that looked like a kind of dune buggy. "Hop in," he said. "We use this to get closer to the different specific digs we're working on—but we still have to do some hiking."

Billy nodded his approval at their mode of transportation. "This is perfect for all these hills and the sandy soil."

Terry let Stego take the driver's seat, but warned him, "We've got city folk here. Better take the longer road, it's not so…so…*surprising*."

David laughed. "That's the first time in my life I've been called *city folk*. Besides, I like *surprising* things."

Stego looked at his dad. His dad looked at Billy, who laughed and said, "A good surprise never hurt nobody."

So, Stego revved the engine and Bekah shouted, "Anyone who falls out has to walk the rest of the way!"

Once they reached *excavation site 3b*, David peeled his fingers off the buggy's side bar. He had been holding on for dear life. It had been a brain-bouncing blast!

Darin hopped out ahead of everyone else and gallantly offered his hand to help Bekah out of the buggy. "You know, Bekah," he said in a grand sort of a way, "I think everyone should call you *Bellasaurus*."

"Wow, Darin, that is, like, so totally sweet," Bekah said, rewarding him with another smile."

David turned to Abel. "Bellasaurus?"

Abel rolled his eyes and whispered, "It means, *beautiful lizard.*

David tried not to laugh out loud.

After a ten-minute hike, the group found themselves looking into a very large hole dug into the side of a reddish sandstone hill—it went both down and back.

Stego and Bekah waved for David and Darin to follow them, and they all tumbled down the sides of the hole and headed back into the hillside.

Billy and Abel stayed up with Terry and Dinah. Billy pulled David's map out of his pocket and showed it to the Soures. "Are any of the landmarks on this map familiar to you?"

Terry took the map and looked it over for a minute, with Dinah peeking over his shoulder. "Look, here, Dinah. This must be Anger Rock, and over here must be Bone Ridge…" He paused to look at Billy. "Yeah, we know where this area is—about a 20 minute ride from the main camp site." Then he asked curiously, "What's *The Fossil They Never Wanted Us to Find*?"

Billy smiled. "We don't know. But, we thought you might like to join us on our treasure hunt."

Dinah reached out to touch the star on the map. "Can't help but think that it's really *The Fossil We Always Wanted to Find*."

****

At 5:00 a.m. the next morning, David, Abel, and Darin all shot through the soft ceiling of their tent as the radio alarm blared out a rowdy country love song. "*I'll never stop lovin' you. 'Till the end of time, that's all I'll ever do…*"

Abel and David dived toward the alarm and started pushing any buttons they could find. Finally, one of them (neither was sure who) succeeded in getting the blaring music to stop. Then they grabbed their pillows, rolled over, and told Darin, "Have fun, lover-boy."

Like lightning, Darin had already dressed while the others had been trying to silence the alarm. Now, he smoothed down his shirt and only paused as he left the tent to stick out his tongue at his companions' comment. He was on his way to meet Bekah, who had asked him to help her make breakfast for everyone.

****

Trying not to look too far down, David followed Rebekah as she led him down the steep side of the canyon, one foothold at a time. It was only 10:00 a.m., but David was already sweating. His body hadn't yet realized that it was no longer in the land of winter and snow. The farther down into the canyon he went, the cooler the air was. It felt good.

Once he reached the canyon floor, David quickly thanked God for keeping him safe. Then, he thanked Bekah for her help. Together, they went over to meet the others who were looking at David's map and discussing which direction they should go.

The canyon they had descended into was about 75 feet wide. However, four channels seemed to converge at their present location. Two of those channels were on the map. The other two were not.

"I just don't know," Terry said with a sigh. "It's possible that two of these channels could have been formed since the time the map was originally drawn." He shook his head. "Or, we could be in the entirely wrong canyon."

"I think this is the right one," Billy encouraged Terry. "So far we've found all the right landmarks." Then he had to admit, "But, it's possible that running water could have messed up the landmarks we're supposed to find down in the canyon itself."

Finally, Stego suggested, "Hey, let's just split up. Two of us can go up each channel. We'll just make sure each pair has someone with one of the Tadue twins' high-tech wrist bands, since our walkie-talkies won't work through these rock walls."

Everyone was eager to continue the hunt, so they divided up. Stego was to go with his mom, Terry with Abel, David with Billy, and, as luck would have it, Bekah was paired up with Darin. Darin's grin stretched from ear to ear.

As each pair started to head out, Terry gave one word of warning. "At the first—I said *first*—sound of thunder, you must start looking for the quickest way out of the canyon. During the summer heat here, thunderstorms pop up, and flash floods aren't uncommon."

David left the flood worries to Billy and ran ahead down their channel in search of any of the landmarks that had been on the map. Nothing seemed to stand out. After about half an hour of excited searching, David slowed down and walked along at a reasonable pace with Billy

"You know, Billy," David began, "I've been thinking. Our *friend* has to be someone who could get close to my backpack…"

"Yeah," Billy nodded. "So, who's been close to your backpack that might be a suspect?"

"Well, just about half of Greenville," David admitted. "I mean, I've had my backpack at school, church, Dr. Ted's museum, and the library—besides at home and my grandparents' house."

Billy had stopped while David was talking. "Look ahead there. It's a big square rock to the right of the channel, just like on the map."

David whooped with excitement and ran ahead as Billy spoke into his *MuF-ToW* band to tell the others of their find. Reaching the boulder, David hurried around it to see if it had an ascendable slope as shown in the map.

But, *Whoa!* David's hair nearly stood up on end as he came face to face with a very large puma. The cat had heard him coming and was waiting. Now, it screamed and leaped down from a ridge on the rock. Instinctively David's arms went up to shield his face. *Wham!* The weight of the cat knocked him flat on his back. Putting up his hands, David grabbed at the fur and skin around the animal's neck to try and keep its teeth from his face. But, with a snarl, the cat's left paw came forward and hit him on the side of the head. The force of the blow was so hard that David felt himself begin to lose consciousness. He felt paralyzed.

Then, suddenly, the cat screamed again and started to turn. But, it couldn't find its footing. Instead, it threw out its paws, trying to find the ground as its whole body went spinning away from its victim.

Billy had grabbed the creature near the base of its tail and had swung it away from David with all his strength. The cat finally found its footing as it came crashing down near the wall of the channel. Spitting and hissing, it turned to face Billy. But, in Billy's hand, the cat saw a huge silver "fang." So, rather than tangle with the man, or his knife, the puma backed away and bounded up the side of the canyon and out of sight.

****

Back at camp, David winced as he tried to sit up. His neck and shoulder muscles were definitely *way* sore. Dinah was sitting next to him, holding a glass of lemonade and some pain-reliever pills. He took the medicine, then reached up to feel the big bandage wrapped around his head.

When David was ready to try to get up to walk around, Abel and Darin came to escort him to the dinner tent. "Looks like it's *David-the-Diehard* this time," Darin said, with only half a smile.

"At least I don't need any stitches," David replied. "And, Dad and Mom sure are great to let me stay here, as long as there are no signs of infection or a concussion."

As everyone sat around the dinner table and talked, Abel stood up and looked to the west. Then, he turned to the others and quoted Christopher Robin. "Tut, tut, looks like rain."

Stego and Bekah jumped up. They saw the obvious dark clouds, too. “No way!” Stego complained. “This could keep us out of the canyons for the rest of the week.”

Everyone looked disappointed. But Billy tried to look on the bright side. “David could use the rest. That cave you all have dug out at site 3b will be both cool and dry—at least compared to the way it’s gonna be out here.”

Terry joined in. “Seems like a good opportunity to get that big femur bone out of the cave wall.”

“Super-fan-taz-cool!” Darin and David said together.

CHAPTER 11

Down in the dugout at site 3b, David stopped scraping the sandstone away from a big rib bone. His head hurt and he needed a break. As he walked around, he ran his hand along the wall of the cave. It seemed like hundreds of bones were jutting out at every angle and in every direction.

Terry stopped working on his own fossil and said, "So far we've found evidence for between 30 and 40 different dinosaurs at this site. This is what we call a fossil graveyard. That's when we find a group of many fossilized animals all together."

Dinah joined in. "There are fossil graveyards all over the world. Most scientists agree that fossil graveyards are the result of some sort of catastrophe. In many cases, even the evolutionists blame the mass death and quick burial on a flood. However, they always make sure to call it a *local flood*."

"Yeah," Billy agreed. "They wouldn't want anyone to think they believe these graveyards were caused by a worldwide Flood."

"From what I understand," David said, "creationists believe that most fossils can only exist because they were quickly buried and then formed into fossils over a relatively short time. But evolutionists say that fossils form over a very long time and don't require quick burial. My science teacher has shown us lots of videos. It's always some poor dinosaur dying by a stream, then decaying, gradually being buried, and then becoming fossilized over the next million years."

Terry laughed. "Yep, they always make sure they put in that *bit* about millions of years." Then, he grew serious. "Really, it's sad. It seems like they're almost desperate. Even when fossil find after fossil find points to rapid burial—and, even when all the recent evidence has proven fossils can form very quickly—still, they have to cling to millions of years. You see, if they let go of their long years, it takes them one step closer to a creator."

Dinah put her arm through her husband's arm and gave it an encouraging squeeze. "To say that they see evidence of a worldwide Flood would take them a giant step closer to the Creator described in the Bible."

Just then, Darin let out a hoot. "Check this out! I just got this jawbone out of the wall…all by myself! Look, it's still got teeth in it." Everyone went over to admire Darin's trophy.

Trophy fever quickly took over and the previous conversation was forgotten until later. It wasn't long before David had chipped and scraped out his large rib bone. He held it up, and the others congratulated him as if he had found a diamond. David couldn't imagine ever getting tired of such fascinating work.

****

However, by their third day in the cave, David *was* tired. He sat at the cave's entrance, watching the ending of yet another thunderstorm, and sighed. After praying (once again) for the rain to stop, he turned back to a small dinosaur leg he had been working on all day.

Billy came over and put his hand on David's shoulder. "So, what do you think of dino-digging now?"

David tried to smile. "Well, I still think it's great…kinda. Anyway, I guess I'd really rather be on our treasure hunt. I mean, this is way cool and all. It's just that it gets kinda boring after a while."

Billy laughed. "I'll bet Terry and Dinah would say the same thing." Then, he added, "Stego went to check out the canyons last night. He said he thinks if it clears up today, we'll be able to go back there by Friday."

"Cool!" David tried to sound positive. But what he was thinking was, "We have to be back in San Juan by Saturday night!"

****

Friday morning at 5:00 a.m., the radio alarm blared out, *"The Stallion and his Mare, the Rabbit and his hare; love is a mystery that's always near…"*

Abel and David were both beating the clock with their pillows before they finally killed it. "Oh, why does this alarm keep waking us before dawn?" David groaned, holding his head.

But Darin was already dressed. And, as he crawled out of the tent to meet Bekah, he was singing to himself, *"The bull and his cow, the boar and his sow; love is a mystery that's happening right now…"*

Once at the canyon, Billy warned the others, "My guess is that *Prince Puma* has his lair somewhere close to where we want to be, maybe right in the very cave we're looking for. So, we're gonna have to stick together. The sight of all of us together should send him running."

Down in the canyon channel, Billy stayed in front of the group, while Terry and Stego guarded the back. It was a pretty long and wet trek. Nobody bothered trying to stay clean or dry. Along the way, they spotted a hare nibbling on little sprouts and caught sight of a red fox running away. Terry pointed out three different snakes (his personal hobby). Abel found part of a dead guanaco, with its long neck and big eyes—probably one of Prince Puma's recent meals. After a while, an interesting conversation cropped up.

"Albert Einstein, Thomas Edison, Isaac Newton, Henry Ford…"

David added to Stego's impressive list: "Thomas Jefferson, Wolfgang Mozart, Richard Strauss, Vincent Van Gogh…"

Rebekah jumped in with, "Jane Austen, Emily Dickinson, and my personal favorite—Carmen Sandiego…"

"Hey," Terry said, "Carmen Sandiego isn't a real person."

But Darin had caught on to the fun, "Bert from Sesame Street…"

"Mr. Spock…" Abel chimed in.

"Oh, I know one," Dinah said. "How about Mork?"

The younger people in the group had big question marks stamped on their faces. "Like, who's Mork?" Bekah asked.

"You know," her mom answered, "Mork…Mork from Ork…Mork and Mindy…you know, the TV show…"

Stego cleared his throat. "Gee, Mom, I guess that one was before our time."

Billy defended Dinah. "How can you all know Spock without knowing Mork?"

Darin shook his head sadly. "Re-runs are very fickle—giving eternal life to some, and leaving others in the grave."

"Anyway," Terry took control of the conversation, "personal diaries, descriptions from close friends, and lots of published materials give good evidence to support the possibility that all these people, at least the *real* ones we've mentioned, most likely had Asperger Syndrome or some traits from the Autism Spectrum."

"Wow," David said to Darin and Abel, "you guys are up there with the greatest minds in history."

"Don't be too impressed, David-dude," Darin said. "It's not like we can take credit for being smart. I mean, we didn't *make* ourselves."

Abel nodded. "Our mom has always been careful to warn us against pride. It's not like we're perfect. Just like you, God is our Creator. We have to make sure we use any gifts He's given us for *His* glory, not our own."

Everybody nodded in agreement.

Then, Billy pointed to the large square boulder about 100 feet ahead of them. Everyone paused, remembering the dead guanaco and the big cat that had killed it. Billy and Terry each lit a flaming torch. Then, on Dinah's cue, the others started making all sorts of strange loud noises as Billy and Terry headed carefully toward the back of the boulder.

Prince Puma was waiting for them on a small ledge in the boulder. However, he did not attack. Instead, he spit and hissed. Billy moved his flaming torch closer to the cat. It backed up, but swiped with its huge paw.

Being careful to leave the cat an obvious escape route, Billy and Terry moved in closer, with the others still making lots of noise. It only took a few seconds for the Prince to give up his throne and run. Down the boulder he bounded, then across the canyon floor and up the seemingly sheer channel wall.

With continued caution, Billy and Terry climbed up the sloping back of the boulder and looked for the triangular opening that the map said would be there.

It was easy to find. The hard part was getting in. Both Terry and Billy were too big. Stego shook his head. Dinah said she wouldn't even try. Darin was ready to impress Bekah, but his shoulders just wouldn't make it through—that meant Abel was out too. So, Bekah winked at David and said, "Last one in is a rotten dino-egg!"

Both squeezed through without too much trouble and found themselves in a dark, stinky cave. "Pee-yew!" David said, shining his flashlight around. The beam showed the cave to be about 20 feet by 12 feet, with the ceiling never more than 5 feet high. The floor was considerably slanted so that high water would never reach the back of the cave.

"I guess this is Prince Puma's lair," Bekah said, holding her nose. Then she pointed her flashlight to an area near the back of the cave. There were several large bones. And, to the side was what looked like half of a dead hare.

"Look there!" David said, pointing his flashlight toward a little nook to the right.

Bekah crawled across the floor to take a closer look. "It looks like something wrapped up in some old blankets," she said, touching a few medium sized bundles. Then she smiled. "David-dude, I think maybe we've found your treasure!"

****

On their way back to base camp, everyone stuffed sandwiches and chips in their mouths. No one wanted to be bothered with eating when they got back. They all wanted to go right to work exploring the treasure.

In the shade of the common tent, everyone began to carefully unroll the bundles. Each bundle held one piece to a puzzle. Arranging and rearranging, Billy and Terry got the pieces in their right positions and all pushed together. Then, everyone took a step back to see what their treasure was.

Stego looked at his dad and said, "This doesn't seem to make any sense."

"It certainly and simply does…if you believe the Bible," Dinah responded.

"Do you think this is really what it looks like?" Bekah asked.

"It looks clear enough to me," Terry said, leaning closer to touch the fossil. "But Dr. Wilcox and his team at the university will have to be the judge of that."

Billy wiped the sweat off his forehead and laughed. "You wouldn't think we'd be so surprised to see something that makes perfect sense according to creation science. But I bet the evolutionists will have plenty to say about it."

"No matter what," Darin said, "this fossil is going to give them one big evolutionary headache!"

David knelt down by the fossil still encased in quite a bit of surrounding sandstone. Whoever had originally found the fossil had already carefully exposed most of the bones. "It looks like some kind of dog skeleton. I guess it had just eaten since it has part of a skeleton in its belly."

David sat back with a deeply disappointed sigh. "I don't see what's so amazing about that. I mean, I'd hardly call that an exciting end to our treasure hunt."

Darin leaned forward and touched the small skeletal remains in the creature's abdominal cavity. "The treasure, David-dude, is what Mr. Mammal had for lunch."

David perked up and looked more closely. "Well, here's its skull. It's kinda weird. Looks like it had a big head with some sort of beak on it."

"It's a psittacosaur," Stego said.

"A dinosaur?" David asked.

"According to evolution," Billy explained, "mammals weren't supposed to be this big during *the age of the dinosaurs*, but this big guy had a dino for lunch. Now, a dinosaur this size with a small mammal in its belly would be no big surprise. But this…"

"…This dino-eating mammal fossil-find," Abel agreed with his brother, "should give evolutionists one big evolutionary headache."

CHAPTER 12

Fossil Formation
(A Worldwide Flood)

by David J. Avila

Introduction

The latest scientific ideas concerning the *formation of fossils and rock layers* show that there are *two* very different theories. Both theories begin with *different assumptions* regarding the formation of fossils and rock layers and then try to make sense out of the same *existing evidence*. A *true* scientist will look closely at both theories to see which one explains the evidence better.

Evolution begins with the assumption that, over hundreds of millions of years, the "first" living cell evolved into the variety of life we see today. Therefore, evolution assumes that the fossils we find buried in rock layers all over the earth are a rock-solid record of millions of years of evolution. Evolutionists begin with this belief and then try to make sense out of the evidence.

Creation begins with the assumption that the Bible is *true* and that God created all things after their kind about 6,000 years ago. Therefore, creation assumes that the fossils we find buried in rock layers all over the earth are a rock-solid record of the worldwide Flood described in the Bible only thousands of years ago. Creationists begin with this belief and then try to make sense out of the evidence.

For this report, I will first look at fossil fish, then at fossil graveyards, and finally at *living fossils*. Through examining this evidence, I will show that fossil formation is best explained by what the Bible calls—a worldwide Flood.

Fish Fossils

[A dying brachiosaurus falls near the bank of a small river. Gentle waves wash the sand up, little by little, covering the remains. Slowly and gradually the sediment layers build up. Then, over millions of years, the bones slowly fossilize as the layers turn to rock. Tens of millions of years later, a paleontologist unearths the fossil dinosaur.]

This makes a nice little time-lapsed video clip on the QLU web site—*but*, is it science or just a belief?

Obviously, fossils exist. In fact, scientists find them all over the world. But how do fossils really form? For decades evolution has taught that fossils take thousands or even millions of years to form. But does the evidence confirm this idea?

Consider the *billions* of fish fossils we find buried in rock layers all over the earth. Many are so well-preserved that they actually show scales and fins. Now, when a fish dies, it does *not* settle calmly on the bottom of the sea waiting to be slowly covered by sediment—little by little, and layer by layer. No, when a fish dies, top-feeding scavengers attack it. Then, whatever is left sinks to the bottom where bottom-feeding scavengers attack it. Finally, oxygen, moisture, and bacteria attack what's left. Evolution's *slow-and-gradual* fossil formation does not explain the evidence—well-preserved fish fossils.

However, a catastrophic worldwide Flood *would* provide the necessary conditions to produce billions of well-preserved fish fossils—quick burial and a rapid hardening of the surrounding sediment. The powerful currents of water flowing across the continents would have been filled with millions of tons of sand and silt. Many fish (and other animals) in the water would have been buried very quickly. The sifting of the debris within these currents would have produced the fine-layered sediment we see. These layers would have quickly begun to harden because of their high mineral content. So, a worldwide Flood would explain the evidence—billions of well-preserved fish fossils found all over the earth.

I also need to mention that observable science shows that fossils and rocks can form *much* more quickly than evolution teaches. A spark plug, dating perhaps as far back as 1950 (that's A.D.) was found encased in solid rock. Obviously, that rock formed in less than 100 years. And a miner's hat was found that couldn't have been more than a couple hundred years old, but it had literally turned to rock. There are many other examples showing that, given the right conditions, fossils and rocks can form and harden quickly.

Fossil Graveyards

Evolutionists use fossils buried within multiple rock layers as evidence that fossilization is a slow and gradual process. *Fossil graveyards*, however, strongly debate this belief. A fossil graveyard is a large collection of fossils found in one place. These "graveyards" are found all over the world. Let's look at two examples and see how they are strong evidence against evolution's claims.

In Russia, more than 300 pareiasaur skeletons were found buried together—in a standing position, with their heads up. Now, evolutionists claim that a centimeter of rock layer is equal to about 1,000 years. Using this method of dating, they estimate that the pareiasaurs were buried about 260 million years ago. *But*, using the same rock-layer dating method, it would have had to have taken about *ten thousand years* for the pareiasaurs to be buried. I can't imagine that they stayed standing there, with their heads up, for ten thousand years, just waiting to be completely buried. No, it's clear that the layers had to have been laid down in a matter of hours, or even minutes. This fossil graveyard points to a quick, catastrophic burial only a few thousand years ago.

In Peru, more than 300 whale fossils were found buried together within a 370-acre area. According to evolution's slow-and-gradual rock formation, these whales were buried over a period of *two million years*, but this doesn't agree with the evidence. When a whale dies, scavengers quickly attack it and it decays. But these fossilized whales were well-preserved and the skeletons were mostly intact. There was *no* evidence of normal decay. It would take rapid burial, in a matter of weeks (not years), to explain the evidence. This contradicts evolution's millions of years of slow-and-gradual fossil formation, but it upholds the Bible's declaration of a worldwide Flood.

Living Fossils

Evolutionists claim that the fossil record laid down in the rock layers supports their theory of millions of years of slow, gradual *change*. Living fossils loudly refute this claim.

Living fossils are plants and animals that were, at one time, believed to have been extinct for hundreds of millions of years (according to evolution's time-scale). But these same plants and animals were then discovered still living today. Examples include the coelacanth fish (believed by evolutionists to have existed for 340 million years), gingko trees (125 million years), and the Wollemi Pine (150 million years).

There are other plants and animals that are common today, but with the discovery of supposedly very old fossils of these plants and animals, scientists now classify them as living fossils. Examples include crocodiles (believed by evolutionists to have existed for 140 million years), horseshoe crabs (200 million years), Neophilia molluscs (500 million years), cockroaches (250 million years), sea turtles (110 million years), and the list goes on.

According to the QLU web site, fossils provide a record of evolution (which means one kind of animal *changing* into another). But the continually growing list of living fossils provides a record of *no change*. A turtle is still a turtle after 110 million years (according to evolution's time-scale), a cockroach is still a cockroach after 250 million years, a fish is still a fish after 340 million years, and a mollusk is still a mollusk after *half a billion years!* This contradicts evolution's millions of years of slow and gradual change, but upholds what the Bible says—that God created all things according to their kind about 6,000 years ago.

Conclusion

Even though they both look at the same evidence, the two scientific theories concerning the formation of fossils are vastly different. Which one really explains the evidence better?

The billions of well-preserved fossil fish all over the world cannot be explained by evolution's slow-and-gradual formation of fossils and rock layers. But a huge global Flood, dumping tons of sand and silt into the oceans, and burying the fish quickly, *would* produce billions of fossil fish buried in rock layers all over the earth.

The many fossil graveyards we find around the world cannot be explained by evolution's slow-and gradual formation of fossils and rock layers. Based on the condition and positions of the fossils themselves, the rock layers they are buried in simply *cannot* represent millions of years. But a huge global Flood sweeping across the continents would have quickly buried these groups of animals, leaving them to fossilize in the quick-hardening sediment layers.

The *living fossils* we find all over the world defy hundreds of millions of years of evolution (change). Instead, they support what the Bible says, that all things were created after their kind, about 6,000 years ago. One-celled organisms did not evolve into the variety of life we see today. Fish have always been fish, reptiles have always been reptiles, and people have always been people.

The fossil evidence simply does not support evolution's belief in slow-and-gradual fossil and rock formation. It does not support millions of years of evolution. The fossils we find buried in rock layers all over the earth are overwhelming evidence of a quick, massive burial in a worldwide Flood. The evidence makes better sense when we begin with what the Bible calls—a worldwide Flood.

****

TO: chance@science.qlu.net
FROM: drevlution@science.qlu.net
RE: principalship of DMS

I have here in front of me, seven science reports by David Avila, the student I have told you about. The first four reports he wrote for my daughter while she was the principal and science teacher here at DMS. The last three he has written for me.

Now, I have spent my entire winter break on your 'grand' million-dollar web site—including hundreds of its suggested links—trying to find satisfactory answers to the questions that this *eighth grader* has raised. Still, I have no valid scientific answers—not even *one.*

This is ridiculous! Have your people ever even looked at what these creationists are claiming? They are raising legitimate doubts about the theory of evolution. They are doing high-level scientific studies that back their Bible-based ideas. They are even finding real concrete evidence that points to a young earth and a worldwide Flood!

Look! My Evolution Foundation donated nearly 25% of the funds that went into the QLU web site. Now, I am having a hard time coming to terms with the fact that—with all its beautiful animation, highly technical language, and masses and masses of scientific data—it can't disprove anything little David Avila has written.

I *am* a scientist. I have studied the sciences—under the best professors—for most of my life. Science has to do with facts, theories, experiments, and evidence. Science means looking objectively at all the evidence and seeing what it points to. Closing your eyes to a certain theory just because you don't like it is neither scientific nor professional (though I must confess that I myself have been guilty of this).

Science is *not* over-imaginative ape-men drawings. It is *not* some famous actor saying he believes in evolution, and something is *definitely not* a scientific fact just

because it appears in *The World of Rational Science's* monthly publication.

At this point, my eighth grade student seems to have a better grip on 'real science' than your highly paid people at QLU.

I guess this is a challenge—*prove me wrong.*

-Ed

PART 4

Money Better Spent

CHAPTER 13

A group of students outside Darwin Middle School milled around, waiting for their rides. A strong, very contagious bacterial infection was spreading through Greenville. So, the School Board decided to close the schools for ten days in an effort to contain it. Not a word of complaint was heard among the celebrating students. Everyone—teachers included—was excited to get a 'second Christmas break.'

"Uh-oh," one of the kids said nervously looking toward the school building. Dr. Lution was heading toward their group. By the time he reached them, only David, Jack and Jill were left. Everyone else had scattered.

Dr. Lution looked at Jack and Jill and said in a principal's tone, "Don't forget your next report is due the day school re-opens. Now, I think I see your mother's van over there." Then, turning to David, he said, "I spoke with your father at lunch time. He has agreed to meet with me at your home to discuss some important issues. So, *I* will be driving you home today."

Jill put her hand over her mouth in horror. But, all the twins could do was give David a final sympathetic wave before leaving to go meet their mom.

Sitting in Dr. Lution's car, David's mouth felt pretty dry. He couldn't think of a word to say. He prayed for God to help him somehow be a positive witness of Jesus.

Dr. Lution himself seemed uncertain about what to say. So, they rode along without saying anything for a few minutes.

Then, through his window, David saw a large bird circling high above a field. "Look!" he said excitedly. "It's an eagle. Do you see it? I've never seen one around here during the winter. I wonder what it's doing here?"

Dr. Lution had immediately slowed the car and was craning his neck to see the bird. Then, he pulled the car to a stop. David could hardly believe it when Dr. Lution jumped out of the car and actually walked into the deeper snow of the fields to see past a tree branch.

"Look at its white head! It's a bald eagle all right!" he shouted enthusiastically. Then, Edward Lution, Ph.D. times three, just stood there, ankle deep in the snow, watching the majestic bird until it flew out of sight.

David looked at his principal, still standing in the snow, and smiled. "Well, sir, you're almost as enthusiastic about eagles as my friend Darin is."

Dr. Lution tramped back to the car, stomping the snow off his shoes. "I can't help it. They seem so strong, so confident, so *free*."

As they pulled back onto the road, David said, "Billy says that God made all His creatures to be strong and confident in the environment He designed them to live in. He says that people are meant to be that way, too."

Dr. Lution shook his head. "I sure don't feel that way. Usually, I feel frustrated and trapped."

"That's because of sin, sir. You know, everyone is trapped by sin—everyone. But God has provided a way to freedom through Jesus Christ. When we put our trust in Him, we can be strong, confident, and *free*."

Dr. Lution looked over at David and smiled. "That's something worth thinking about."

David smiled back and nodded. For the first time ever, he felt comfortable with Dr. Lution. Then, looking out the window, David caught a final glimpse of the eagle, and silently thanked God for answering his prayers.

******

Behind a large evergreen bush, David and Darin wrestled over the bionic binoculars as quietly as possible. Abel commentated in a whisper, "David has both hands on the binoculars. Well, now, Darin has pulled them loose and nearly has them under his coat. Uh-oh, David has Darin flat on his back. I think this could be it, folks…"

"Time out!" Darin squeaked as he saw a handful of snow coming toward his face. Then, sitting up, Darin continued in a very dignified manner. "Now, David, while it is obvious that I could easily win this fight, I have been holding myself back, due to your head injury."

Then, with mock graciousness, Darin held out the binoculars and said, "Seeing that you are in such a weakened condition, I am willing to let you use my binoculars for the sake of fulfilling our present mission."

Abel smirked. "Yeah, right. He's in such a weakened condition that he was about to whitewash your face."

David took the binoculars with a chuckle. "You really should make another pair of these things."

Darin pouted. "Well, duh! I would if I could…"

David turned to Abel, "Why can't he?"

"Mr. Genius, here, was so juiced up on *Cola Super Max* the night he finally finished them that he doesn't really even know how he got them to work."

David put on a mock expression of horror. "Darin and *Cola Super Max*! That is one scary combination. I'll bet you were practically super-sonic."

Darin stood up with a silly grin. "Yeah…I used to have lots of fun with caffeine. But, once mom discovered I was only sleeping four hours each night, she put a super max *ban* on any and all caffeine—no exceptions."

Abel cleared his throat. "Men, I think we've gotten distracted from the important mission before us. There is still a mutant strain of bacterial slime awaiting neutralization. Don't forget that it's up to us to save Greenville from its slimy disgustingness."

Darin and David both snapped to attention. David set the bionic binoculars to their *topographical scan* setting—to enhance any footprint depressions. Right away, he saw a set of clean tracks leading up Maple Hill. "Looks like it's headed toward the meat shed again," David guessed.

"Perfect, perfect!" Darin rubbed his hands together gleefully. "Our trap is just to the left of the shed." Then he added informatively, "Bacteria love to infest raw meat."

"Hmmm," Abel wondered out loud, "I wonder how bacterial slime feels about frozen pizza and chicken nuggets…since that's about all we have in the freezer up there."

"Well, we're not going to let this mutant monster have a chance to find out."

Step-by-step, little-by-little, the three friends worked their way up toward the meat shed. Finally, they were in place and ready for action.

All of a sudden, they heard an angry roar. Crashing and thrashing sounds came from the far side of the shed. All three hunters broke out of their hiding places to secure their catch. But, just as they came around the corner, a large net dropped on top of *them*.

"Retreat! Retreat!" Darin shouted in a panic. But it was too late. Before they could get untangled from the net, Billy had deftly pulled the net under their six kicking feet and tied the ends together with a thick rope.

"Looks like this bacterial slime monster mutated into something smarter than you expected," Billy laughed. Then he walked over to a tree about 50 feet away, stuck his pocket knife into it, and told them, "Here's a knife to cut yourselves free." Looking at the trapped trio, Billy smirked, "I'd love to stay and see you guys inch your way over to that tree, but I've got to get this pizza in the oven."

****

Sitting back in the Maple Hill cabin, David scarfed down a piece of pizza as he told the others about Dr. Lution's discussion with his father.

"I guess Dr. Lution kinda wanted my dad to show him some sort of tangible *facts* that would prove *unquestionably* that God is real. My dad told him that even scientists have to rely on faith."

David popped three mini carrots into his mouth, and continued, "I even quoted Hebrews 11:1 to him, 'Now faith is confidence of what we hope for and assurance about what we do not see.'" After swallowing, David continued. "I thought he might get mad at that, but instead, he just nodded his head."

"Looks like the Lord's tuggin' at Edward Lution's heart, just like he did his daughter's," Billy said with an excited grin.

"I hope he defects to creation's side, too," Darin said, grabbing a handful of grapes. "He's been fighting on the wrong side for long enough."

"Well," Abel said, holding up David's notebook, "from the looks of this next report topic, he hasn't joined our side, yet—*The Benefits of Evolution Today*."

"Yeah," David sighed. "Dr. Lution's all into how evolution research is the key to modern medical breakthroughs. I guess his wife died of cancer a long time ago."

Billy's amber eyes misted over as he said quietly, "No one can fathom the pain of a broken heart."

David wasn't sure what to say. Then Darin changed the suddenly somber mood by grunting and pointing to his overstuffed, drooling mouth. He was holding up both hands. On one hand he held up two fingers. On the other hand he held up all five fingers.

"Whoa!" David said in a tone of genuine admiration. "Twenty-five grapes. I don't think I've ever gotten more than twenty-two."

But Abel was more suspicious, "I'll bet you picked out all the smallest ones..."

Billy slapped his hand to his forehead. "You guys are crazy! Get out of here and go play while I get some work done." Nobody was gonna argue with that. So, they threw on their coats, hats, boots, and gloves, and headed out the door and down to the frozen waters under Rocky Creek Bridge.

Darin had just suggested a rump-sliding contest when they heard the sound of an approaching vehicle. Scurrying along the ice as fast as possible, the three friends dived under the cover of the bridge and began to set up an ambush. Darin and Abel quickly made snowballs, while David tried to get himself into a position where he could see the approaching car.

The vehicle slowed down and stopped before crossing the bridge. The boys crawled up with as many snowballs as they could hold. Then, *"Fire!"* They started pelting anything and anyone that was on the road before them.

Three of the snowballs made contact with a dark green SUV. Then, the driver's door quickly slammed shut and whoever had been about to get out of the car sent snow and gravel flying in his anxiousness to escape.

David grabbed Darin's arm. "Man, you're not gonna believe this. But, that's the same SUV Billy and I saw on Canton Road—you know, when we got that information about all that fake ape-man stuff. I'll bet he was gonna put something in the mailbox."

"Aw! What a blatantly big ballistic blunder!" Darin looked tragic. "I'll bet Billy's gonna be ballistically bummed."

Up at the cabin, Billy was pretty disappointed that the boys had missed their chance to find out who their *friend* was. He just said, "Well, maybe next time."

Then the phone rang, and the boys grabbed a few cookies and started to head back out for a rowdy rump-race. But, Billy stopped them as he hung up the phone. "Guess what. We've just been invited to QLU's *Center for Disease Control and Research*. We need to be there by 2:30."

"Who invited us?" Darin asked grabbing the last cookie.

Billy smiled, "Dr. E. V. Lution, Ph.D. times three."

CHAPTER 14

Dr. Lution was waiting for Billy and his gang in the first floor lobby of Quantum Leap University's Center for Disease Control and Research. After signing in at a very official looking front desk, they were sent on up to the second floor lobby. There, Dr. Lution spoke to a uniformed security guard who nodded and made a phone call. While waiting, Billy pointed out a large picture on one of the walls. It was an enlarged photo of the Center's opening celebration.

"Hey, Dr. Lution, sir!" David said in surprise. "Look, that's *you* cutting the ribbon."

Dr. Lution blushed, looking both pleased and a bit uncomfortable. "Yes, David. The Lution Foundation provided a large percentage of the funding necessary to build this center."

"Way cool!" David said, impressed.

"Uh, then, why didn't they name the building after you?" Darin asked without realizing that it wasn't the most appropriate question.

Dr. Lution laughed. "Well, Darin, the money that my foundation raises is from thousands of people all over the world, not just myself."

"I guess that's true," Abel replied. Then, he added, "But I don't understand why an *evolution* foundation would help fund the building of a disease research center."

"That's what we're here to find out," Dr. Lution said. Then he turned to introduce the stranger who was walking toward their group. "This is Professor Chance Nottah. He is in charge of the research department here at QLU."

Dr. Nottah greeted them all with a stiff sort of bow. Then he turned specifically to David and looked him up and down. "Humph!" the fifty-something red-haired professor grumped. "So, you're the boy who's been causing all this trouble." He took a step closer to David, and David took a step back. "When we're done here, young man, you'll realize that it's people like your friend here," he gestured toward Billy, "that are slowing down the train of scientific progress."

Dr. Nottah took another step toward David and opened his mouth to say more. But Billy stepped between them and said in a firm tone, "Sir, if you have a problem with what *people like me* are doing, then you should be speaking to *me.*"

"Okay," Dr. Nottah said, taking up the challenge. "You *creationists* are giving us regular Christians a bad name." Pointing a finger at Billy, he continued, "I'm a Christian. I go to church, but you don't see me mixing my science with my faith. God didn't intend for us to take the Bible literally. He intended for us to use the brains he gave us!"

Dr. Lution coughed and said a bit uncomfortably, "Chance, why don't we just go up to the labs as we planned."

Dr. Nottah and Billy stared each other down with arms folded across their chests. Then Dr. Nottah said, "Anyway, in our labs you will all see irrefutable evidence that a growing knowledge of evolution is the key to scientific advancement." Looking at Billy, he added, "Even *you*, Mr. James, will have no choice but to be convinced." Then he led them toward the elevators.

David leaned toward Abel and Darin and whispered, "Do you really think he has *irrefutable evidence*?"

Abel shook his head and whispered back, "Chance Nottah?—Not-a-chance!"

Darin and David both busted out in a coughing fit trying to cover their laughter at Abel's pun. It was so obvious, that Dr. Lution tried to cover for them by asking, "Are you okay? If either of you is sick, we should postpone this trip as you could spread an infection in the labs."

David and Darin wiped their eyes and tried to look very healthy. "Really, sir," David said, "we're fine. Really."

Dr. Lution smiled at their antics, but Dr. Nottah just rolled his eyes as he pressed the elevator button.

In the fourth floor lobby, each person in the group was given a large I.D. tag to wear around their necks. They were also given a radiation monitor to clip onto their belt loops. Then, they were required to leave their cell phones and any other such devices at the desk.

"Man!" Darin grumbled. "Bekah's supposed to call today. I don't want to miss her call."

David and Abel giggled and poked Darin in the ribs, chanting, "Darin and Bekah sittin' in a tree…"

Nearly an hour later, the group was heading into a *third* laboratory. David tried hard to hide a yawn. Then he whispered to Abel, "Talk about boring. Blah, blah, blah. This is exactly how Jack and Jill described their visit to QLU."

"So, David," Dr. Lution asked, trying to regain David's attention, "do you have any questions for Dr. Nottah before he shows us around this lab?"

David felt put on the spot, but tried to come up with a good question. "Well, Dr. Nottah, you've shown us several examples of different bacteria and viruses mutating and changing. But, could you please explain where the evolution part comes in."

The professor responded, "I would think that the answer would be obvious." Then he began to explain. "In these labs, you have seen with your own eyes that bacteria can mutate and change—not just once, but many times over thousands of generations. They are going from one strain of bacteria that is easily treated, to what is almost a whole new strain, one that is nearly impossible to treat with current medicines." He crossed his arms and concluded, "That *is* evolution."

David shook his head, and said, "Well, no, sir. From what I've been taught in science class, that is *not* evolution."

Dr. Nottah's lips tightened as he shot a dirty look at Dr. Lution, David's current science teacher.

Dr. Lution felt irritated at his colleague's attitude, but was impressed with David's understanding. He had a hard time refraining from a smile as he responded, "Um, Chance, I think David is referring to the fact that all the examples we have seen are copying errors of existing genetic information, while evolution requires genetic change leading to new, complex systems."

Dr. Nottah bit his lip, then answered, "Well, even if all *these* examples involve degraded information, it is obvious from the diversity of plant and animal life around us that genetic change has produced countless new complex systems during the past 4 billion years." Then, he looked at Billy and said, "Mr. James, wouldn't you agree that the small changes we observe through mutations today could certainly produce a lot of change over 4 *billion* years?"

Billy remained polite as he answered. "Professor, *if* the changes we observed today were leading to new, complex systems, given billions of years, I might agree. However, from a purely *scientific* view, this type of change has *never* been observed. It is only a belief outside of operational science."

Dr. Nottah took a deep breath and let it out slowly, then burst out, "Look around you. Look, look, look! Everything you see is *purely scientific proof* that new systems have been produced by mutations and that living things have evolved."

"Show me your so-called *proof*," Billy challenged. Dr. Lution leaned in, eager to hear the answers and see the outcome of this debate. Darin, Abel and David, however, felt a bit uncomfortable, so, spotting a vending machine down the hall, they escaped in that direction.

"Hello!" Dr. Nottah said in frustration. "Look at this building, it was designed and built by intelligent creatures—not single-celled, brainless blobs. We are here as the direct result of evolution."

Billy said, "I totally agree that people are wonderfully amazing and intelligent beings. I just absolutely disagree with the belief that humans *evolved* from single-celled, brainless blobs. *Science* says 'No! The type of change evolution needs has never been observed.' There are only copying mistakes and sorting of information—no evolution!"

"What are you talking about?" Dr. Nottah slapped the wall in frustration. "Obviously, there *must* be genetic change producing new, complex systems! Even if we *never* see it in a laboratory, we know it exists. If it didn't exist, we would all still be single-celled, brainless blobs."

"Professor," Billy said, "brainless blobs will always be brainless blobs, because that is what they have always been. Your mutating bacteria will always be bacteria." He paused to let that sink in. Then he said, "In the same way, people will always be people, because that is what we have always been."

Dr. Nottah threw up his hands and raised his voice, "You are making no sense. Are you saying that we just appeared here? Zap! There we were, fully human?"

Dr. Lution stepped forward and put his hand on his friend's arm. "Yes, Chance," he said in a serious tone, "that is *exactly* what Mr. James is saying—people did not evolve from blobs. He is saying that we were created human—and, not just as a trillion cells that somehow all work well together, but as beings that think, feel, reason, remember, and make choices."

"Well, of course we think and feel. That is all part of *survival of the fittest*—all part of evolution." Dr. Nottah insisted.

"Chance?" Dr. Lution shook his head. "A series of spelling errors will never produce a novel. Millions of mathematical mistakes will never produce a functioning cell phone. Likewise, there is no way that even a billion years of mutations, copying errors, could have accidentally, just by random chance, formed something even as comparatively simple as that potted plant over there. If not that plant, then how could it have managed to form the person who took pleasure in the plant and brought it here so that he could enjoy it while he worked out the mysteries of the universe?"

Dr. Nottah looked at Dr. Lution and said with astonishment, "*Edward!* What are you saying? Don't tell me that you are agreeing with this man…that you are becoming a…a *creationist*."

Dr. Lution started to answer, but was interrupted by a loud commotion down the hall. A second later, David was running toward them. "Quick!" he said to Billy. "The snack machine ate all our money, and now it's eating Darin!"

At the end of the hall, they found Darin with his arm stuck in the *mouth* of the vending machine. Darin looked up at all the faces staring down at him and tried to look innocent. "Uh, I was just trying to get my pack of milk chocolate smothered marshmallow chocolate chip cookie cakes…"

CHAPTER 15

Sitting at a table in *The Library of Secular Science*, Jack whispered to David, "You'll never guess who Jill and I saw in here the other day."

"Who?" David asked with interest.

"It was Dr. Ted Veritas…" Jack started to answer.

"And you'll never guess what he was doing," Jill interrupted.

"What?" David asked with even greater interest.

"He was meeting with Miss Abbi…alone…in the kids' story time play area."

David wasn't impressed. "So? He was probably just asking her a question while she prepared for the next group of kids."

"He was playing the guitar…" Jack said.

"*What*?" David exclaimed.

"He was singing…" Jill added.

"*Singing*?" David raised his voice. "No way!"

"Shhhh!" Jack and Jill shushed him.

"Your heart beat is calling to me…" Jack crooned softly.

"Only in your arms will I be free…" Jill sang, putting her hand over her heart.

"But, I mean, well, you know, Miss Abbi seems to be, you know, leaning toward creationist views now," David argued.

"Dr. Ted doesn't seem to mind," Jill giggled.

****

When Mrs. Hill dropped David off at home, Corina, his older sister, handed him a 9 by 12 inch box with his name on it. "What's this?" David asked.

Cory just shrugged. "I don't know. I don't open other people's mail. But," she added, "I do know that a man in a blue coat, with glasses, driving a dark green SUV put it in our mailbox at exactly 2:10 this afternoon."

"A green SUV?" David shouted excitedly.

"Uh, yeah. Do you know who it was?" she asked curiously.

David shook his head, but couldn't hide his smile as he ran upstairs to look at the new information his *friend* had for him today.

****

In the science section of the QLU library, Billy James headed way back among the big musty-smelling scientific journals. He was hoping to find a few journals that would back up the conclusions he and the Tadue twins had come to in their recent research.

"Hello, Mr. James," Dr. Lution said, coming up behind Billy. "I was hoping for an opportunity to speak with you, uh, without the others around."

Billy smiled and said, "Would you like to go and sit down in a quiet corner?"

Seated in two comfortable reading chairs, the men discussed many different issues concerning creation science research and weighed facts and theories for nearly 20 minutes. Billy could tell that what they were talking about wasn't really what was on Dr. Lution's mind. Finally, Dr. Lution stopped talking and just stared out the window for a minute. Billy quietly left him to his thoughts.

Then, Dr. Lution took a deep breath and began, "Billy, obviously, as a scientist, I have been brought around to seeing things from your scientific view point. Where I am having trouble is on a different level. To agree with creation science, I must believe in a creator. Of course, many scientists are joining the Intelligent Design bandwagon. However, to believe in the God of the Bible, is something much bigger…"

He took another breath and let it out slowly. Then, looking Billy right in the eye, he asked slowly, "Why would God let my wife die such a slow and painful death? Why?"

Billy took off his cap with a sigh. Leaning back in his chair, he looked at the shelves around them. Then, leaning forward, he looked right at Dr. Lution. "Death is the most awful, incomprehensible, terribly sad thing of all. To us, it's the end."

Dr. Lution closed his eyes and wiped a tear from his face.

"But, Edward," Billy continued earnestly, "suffering and death were *not* a part of God's original plan. God created a paradise—with no suffering and no death."

Dr. Lution opened his eyes and drew his brows down. "Then why is suffering all around us? Why is death everywhere?"

Billy leaned forward even more. "Sin, Edward. Sin is why there's suffering and death. People, even non-believers, want to blame God when they suffer. But they have it backwards. We ourselves—our sin—is to blame for our suffering. God is not the tyrant some people make him out to be. No, God is *love*.

"While He was without sin—God Himself became a man and suffered the worst kind of death. He died to redeem us from the curse of our sin, and to allow us to regain true paradise. He died to give your wife eternal life. And He died…to give *you* eternal life."

Dr. Lution leaned back in his chair and stared at the ceiling, his body tense with uncertain hope. But, after a short moment, the tension was gone. Closing his eyes, Dr. Lution slowly nodded to himself. This was right—this was a truth that encompassed both the tangible and the intangible.

Seeing the peace of a "secure hope" come across his new friend's face, Billy quietly stood up and left Edward Victor Lution to consider this new hope he was now accepting as the foundation of the rest of his life.

****

Up on Maple Hill, David, Abel and Billy went through the new pile of articles from their *friend.*

"Did you see this one?" David asked in an excited voice. *"152 million dollars spent on evolution TV mini-series.*"

"Look at this!" Abel broke in. "*$60,000.00 per minute to produce a 30 minute animated film on evolution for the high school classroom.*" He opened his big eyes all the way and emphasized, "that was $60,000.00 *per minute.*"

David shook his head. "Whoa! That's like double what my dad makes in a *year*—just in one *minute*!"

"Check this out," Billy said holding up an article. "*Over one million dollars spent on Quantum Leap University's new evolution web-site.*"

"Uh-oh, look at this," David said. *"Tenured math professor let go after questioning the basis of the big bang.*"

Abel grabbed the next article. "*Christian college professors claim science research grants unfairly distributed to secular universities.*"

David read, "*New radiometric dating department opens*. The University president is quoted, *'An excellent use of*

118 million dollars of federal money'—that's *tax-payers'* money!"

Billy tossed the articles in his hand back onto the coffee table in frustration. "Evolution is hailed as making great advancements in science, but all it's really doing is sucking up all the tax dollars and donations for…well, for self-promotion. That's money that should have been used strictly for medical research."

Suddenly, the door burst open and Darin came rushing in. "Hey, dudes, you'll never guess who I saw with Dr. Ted Veritas at Biggie Burgers!"

"Abbi Informed?" David guessed. "They're in love, you know."

Everyone turned to stare at David in surprise.

But, after blinking six or seven times, Darin said, "No… It was Dr. Ed Lution. Man, you should have seen them." He chuckled at the memory. "They were throwing their hands and arms around like umpires. Their voices were going up and down and all around. Unfortunately, I couldn't make out much of what they were saying. I couldn't even tell if they sounded more excited or mad."

"Interesting…" Billy said thoughtfully.

****

Three days later, David and the gang all sat together staring at each other in disbelief. Darin had just gotten off the phone with Rebekah Soure, who had had some disturbing news.

Although the Soures had tried to keep their dino-eating mammal fossil a secret until official testing could be done, a nearby secular university had found out about it. Now, all the news sources were full of headlines like *Ridiculous Fossil-Fake*, *Re-worked Fossil Misinterpreted*, and *Desperate*

Creationist Hoax. Then, a ruling had been passed down that said, unless legitimate documentation of the original 1967 excavation could be presented, the fossil would be confiscated for government testing.

Darin moaned. "Man, there's no doubt that if the evolutionists do *their* testing on it, that fossil's sure to be declared a fraud." Then, he growled, "It's just not fair!"

"Well, Darin," Billy said, standing up, "I understand how you feel. But we need to remember that our faith doesn't stand on a certain piece of evidence—it stands on the Word of God."

Putting on his hat, Billy continued. "Think about it this way—before we found that fossil, we believed what the Bible says, that all the land animals were created on day six and lived together. What if our dino-eating mammal fossil-find is found to be nothing more than a fake? Is that going to change what we believe? *No*. The truth remains the truth, whether or not this fossil turns out to be the *real thing*.

Then, grabbing his coat, he added, "But, now's not the time to talk about all that. Right now we need to find some *legitimate documentation* for that dig."

Pulling on his own coat, Abel asked, "Where are we going?"

David chimed in, "What are we gonna do?"

Billy's eyes sparkled with anticipation as he explained, "Looks like we're gonna have to set a trap and catch that *friend* of ours."

The first one out the door was Darin. "Oh, boy!" he shouted, "setting traps is what Darins do the bestest!"

****

From high up in the big pine tree by Lonely Road Bridge, Abel spotted the green SUV approaching. Hearing

Abel's signal, David and Billy scrambled to pull the thin, but bushy tree across the road. While they ran back to hide, Darin (dressed in winter-camouflage) was about ten feet above them, inching his way out onto a sturdy oak branch, ready to snap the *tell-tale* pictures.

Seeing the "fallen" tree across the road, the SUV slowed to a stop. The driver's door opened. A man wearing a hat and a blue coat climbed out and walked over toward the roadblock.

Inch by inch…Darin was almost right above the man. Just a few more inches.

But suddenly, Darin felt himself slipping. Silently, he grabbed for a branch above him. As it slipped through his hands, he wrapped his legs around the branch he was on. In one smooth motion, he found himself hanging upside down, with his face about one foot in front of their secret *friend*. "Smile!" Darin said, as he snapped three consecutive pictures from his inverted position.

But then the branch began to bend. Darin's arms began to flap. "Heee-yelp!" he screamed. Grabbing for anything that might save him, Darin ended up wrapped around the man from the SUV. Together they tumbled to the snowy ground.

Billy and David ran out of their hiding place. Abel climbed out of the pine and a woman hopped hurriedly out of the SUV. Darin fumbled and tumbled around, but finally managed to pull the man's hat off to get a good look at his face. "Oh, like, totally blow my mind! Our *friend* really is our friend. It's Dr. Teddy!"

Dr. Theodore Veritas disengaged himself from Darin and stood up. Abigail Informed ran to his side and began brushing the snow off his coat.

By this time, Billy was standing in front of Dr. Ted with a smile that stretched from ear to ear. Reaching out to shake

Dr. Ted's hand, Billy said, "It is my pleasure to welcome you—both of you—to our side of the battle for truth. And, thank you for all the information you've already found for David."

Dr. Ted shook Billy's hand heartily, and laughed. "It's been a grand adventure, my friend."

Darin was backing up snapping pictures of Dr. Ted whose arm was protectively around Abigail Informed. Then, he started singing, "Teddy and Abbi, sitting in a tree, k-i-s-s-i-n-g. First comes love, then comes marriage…" But, Darin's sassy little song came to a sudden and violent end as David and Abel pounced on him and buried him in a snowdrift.

CHAPTER 16

The Benefits of Evolution Today (Money Better Spent)

by David J. Avila

Introduction

Evolution claims to be a science that benefits mankind today. Evolutionists give examples from medicine, agriculture, and other areas to show the wonderful 'benefits' of applied evolution. Then they boldly warn that rejecting evolution (by accepting creation) would put a halt to these scientific advances. But a closer look will show that it is actually evolution itself that is slowing the 'train of scientific progress.'

Evolution begins with the assumption (belief) that all the species we see today evolved from a single-celled organism. Evolution claims that the *small* changes we observe today (mutations and natural selection) have produced the *big* changes (evolution) over billions of years. Evolutionists claim that this theory is the foundation of modern biology, and is benefiting mankind today.

Creation begins with the assumption (belief) that God created all living things according to their kind—each loaded with genetic information. Creation claims that the *small* changes we observe today (mutations and natural selection) have produced amazing variation and adaptability within the created kinds. Creationists claim that the study of mutations and natural selection (not evolution) can and does greatly benefit mankind.

For this report, I will first show the difference between *change* and *evolution*. Then I will look at some of the claimed "benefits of evolution" and show that they are not really *evolution* at all. Finally, I will show that the latest scientific advances in genetic information that are benefiting mankind today are in perfect agreement with creation science and the Bible.

Evolution or Change

Both evolution and creation agree that we observe changes in genetic information (DNA). Evolutionists claim that these changes are *evolution*. But there is a difference between *change* and *evolution*. The changes we *do* see come from mutations and natural selection—copying mistakes and sorting of genetic information. We do not see evolution—genetic changes that produce new, complex systems and organisms. Evolution says that the "first" single-celled organism changed, over time, into organisms with eyes, bones, hearts, scales, fins, legs, and so on. However, the first cell did not have all this extra information within itself. It had to be added. Evolution claims that mutations and natural selection are producing the information for those new, complex systems.

Creationists claim that God did not start with a single cell, but rather, created living things according to their kind, each with a vast amount of genetic information within them. This would allow for variety and adaptation. Creation claims that the changes we see are information being sorted (through natural selection) or information being changed by copying errors (through mutation). But information for complex, new systems is not being produced through mutation and selection—no evolution. So which claim best fits the evidence?

Mutations are changes within the genetic information of a single organism. When a cell reproduces, a copy of its DNA is made. Sometimes there is a copying error, called a mutation. Usually, mutations are harmful—a beetle born without wings would have trouble finding a mate or avoiding a predator. However, occasionally, a mutation turns out to be beneficial—a beetle born without wings on a very windy island wouldn't fly and would, therefore, be less likely to be blown out to sea. But, whether harmful or helpful, mutations have never *(ever)* been observed to produce the genetic information necessary for new, complex systems and organisms.

Natural selection is the other "tool" of change that both creationists and evolutionists observe at work. Natural selection is a change in the genetic information of a group of organisms (rather than a single organism). If a group of beetles were reproducing on a windy island, the few beetles that have no wings (caused by mutation) would be *more fit* to survive and reproduce. So the next generation would have more wingless beetles. Natural selection would eventually make a large population of wingless beetles on this windy island. But, no new complex systems are being produced—natural selection is only operating on existing systems.

Every scientist agrees that we observe changes in living organisms—the result of mutations and natural selection. But *no* scientist has observed even one case of mutations and selection producing the type of genetic information necessary for new, complex systems and organisms.

Therefore, since evolution cannot occur without *this* kind of change, evolution does *not* fit the evidence.

Example from Medicine

The QLU evolution web site claims that the theory of evolution has produced many outstanding benefits in the practice of medicine. One of their favorite examples is the understanding of the "evolution" of bacterial resistance to antibiotics.

When antibiotics were first used to treat diseases, they had great success. However, over time, many strains of bacteria changed and became resistant to certain antibiotics. That's because the antibiotic *(acting like natural selection)* kills most of the bacteria, but the resistant bacteria *(more fit)* survive. These resistant bacteria then reproduce to make more resistant bacteria (just like the wingless beetles). When the antibiotic is used again, there are many more resistant bacteria that survive and reproduce. Soon, the antibiotic has no effect, because most of the bacteria are resistant.

The web site goes on to suggest various strategies to treat bacterial infections "based on evolutionary theory." (1) Don't use antibiotics to treat viral infections. The antibiotics won't kill the virus, but it will kill off nonresistant bacteria, leaving more resistant bacteria to reproduce. (2) Avoid mild doses of antibiotics. A weak dose could leave bacteria that are somewhat resistant. These will reproduce and be harder to fight next time. (3) The treatment of a bacterial infection should be long enough to cause the extinction of the illness-causing bacteria.

This is actually very sound advice for any doctor to follow, but it's *not* based on evolution. It's true that a mutation could cause some bacteria to be resistant to antibiotics, but that mutation is *not* producing a new, complex system, it's actually operating on an existing system—*no* evolution. And it's true that a mild or short dose of antibiotic would kill off many bacteria, but leave the resistant bacteria to reproduce. This is similar to natural selection (with the antibiotic selecting for resistant bacteria) but it is *not* producing new systems—*no* evolution. Evolutionists claim this, and other medical research, as one of the benefits of evolution. But, actually, this research has nothing to do with evolution. The bacteria is still, and always will be, bacteria.

Examples from Agriculture

The science textbook at Darwin Middle School also claims benefits of evolution—this time in agriculture. Corn is a good example. Viruses can do serious damage to corn crops. According to the science book, an "evolutionary perspective" pointed scientists to a wild variety of corn that is resistant to the damaging viruses. By combining genes from this wild variety of corn with domestic corn, they developed virus-resistant domestic corn. But again, this has nothing to do with evolution. In reality, during its many years of domestication, the corn had *lost* genetic information—the genes that made it resistant to the virus. So scientists added the lost information back in to the domestic corn. This was not a spontaneous appearance of new genetic information (as evolution would require), it was sorting and selecting (with the scientists' help) information that was already there—*no* evolution.

Conclusion

Evolution claims to be a science benefiting mankind today. But the evolutionists don't have even one example of evolution—genetic change producing new, complex systems—on their side. Their examples are all dealing with copying mistakes, sorting information, or reintroducing genetic information that already exists. These processes are not leading to the new, complex systems necessary for evolution to be true—they're only changing systems that already exist.

It is true that the study of genetic information is greatly benefiting mankind today. But it has nothing to do with evolution. It does, however, have everything to do with creation science and the Bible. God created plants and animals, each according to their kinds—complete with a vast amount of genetic information that would allow for variety and adaptation. The study of mutations and natural selection can greatly benefit mankind today. It is like unwrapping God's secret gift—hidden genetic information—and using it for the common good of all.

Evolution, on the other hand, has produced no benefit to mankind. If anything, it is evolution that has slowed the 'train of scientific progress.' It misinterprets the evidence and biases scientists against the facts. On top of this, it is 'stealing' private and federal funds away from truly beneficial scientific research. The $60,000 per minute spent on the EPM animated high school evolution DVD could have been better spent on flu research and vaccine production. The 1.2 million dollars spent on the QLU evolution web site could have been better spent in research for the cure of cancer. In addition, the 152 million dollars spent on the popular evolution mini-series could have been much better used in agricultural genetic research. All of this money could have been better spent on research to benefit mankind.

****

To: evalution@science.qlu.net
From: drevlution@science.qlu.net
RE: Principalship of DMS

My dear daughter, Evangeline,

School has been open for a week now and you'll never guess what. I've been released from my position (fired)! The School Board held an emergency meeting over the weekend and concluded that I was "not fit at this time to continue as principal of Darwin Middle School."

I wasn't surprised, but I was angry. It's ridiculous! They wouldn't even listen to the sound scientific evidence I presented to defend my new beliefs. They had already made their decision before the meeting was even called. It was all just a formality. Anyway, I now see what I must have sounded like to you just a few months ago.

On a more positive note—you'll like this—I've decided to let the Lution Evolution Foundation funds run dry on previous financial agreements. Then, I will officially close the foundation.

Starting next week, I plan to start investing my own personal funds into a new project. It turns out that Dr. Theodore Veritas (and his fiancée, Abigail Informed) have been going through the same changes in their beliefs as I have. So, Dr. Ted and I have decided to combine resources and turn his *Museum of UNcertain Science* into a museum for creation science. I must admit, we're pretty excited. I feel happier than I have in 30 years. I have even found peace concerning your beautiful mother's death. Yes, God is good.

I suppose you can guess who will be taking my position as principal of DMS—Professor Chance Nottah. I'm sure you remember him from your years at QLU. It seems the

'giants' David has to fight just keep getting bigger. But, God will always be bigger still. So, I'm guessing Chance is going to have a very *enlightening* time at DMS.

Please give my best regards to Cliff Newman. Tell him that when he has a few days off, I'd like to meet him.

With my love,

Dad

P.S. I've decided to take you up on getting myself tested for Asperger Syndrome. It can't hurt, and it could answer a lot of questions…

A NOTE FROM DAVID

Hola Amigos!

This is David Avila. I thought I'd share a couple more important things I've learned this school year.

First, I know what it's like to be afraid and discouraged. It's natural to feel intimidated when authority figures (like teachers) disagree with you. But, don't be afraid. Remember when young David decided to fight Goliath? His older brothers and even the king told him that he could never beat the giant. But David trusted the Lord and won the victory. Also, keep in mind that not all battles are won in a day. Just keep a humble, prayerful attitude, making sure you speak to others respectfully—just as you want them to speak to you.

Second, don't be afraid to admit it when you don't have all the answers. One time, when I was having a discussion, someone brought up an issue I'd never even heard of. I could have tried to bluff my way through. But bluffing is about the same as lying—it just causes problems later. It's always best to be up front and honest. You can say something like, "Well, I haven't had a chance to read about the creationist's view on that issue. Give me some time to look into it."

Misericordia!

David

ABOUT THE AUTHORS

John is a nationally certified middle school teacher. He has worked with teenagers for the past 20 years, both as a teacher and as a youth pastor. Lisa received her college degree in English Literature. She has also been active working with youth for the past 20 years. The Foxes live on a ten-acre farm in Central Ohio where they homeschool their six children. They also own lots of dogs and a variety of fun farm animals.

Authors' Note

Although this book is a work of fiction, the scientific evidence discussed is *real* and is available to everyone. Evolution's bold 'scientific' claims have clear religious implications against faith in God and His Word. Our goal is simply to provide real scientific evidence that refutes evolution's claims and upholds the Word of God from beginning to end. We encourage our readers to ask questions and to do further research.

Always remember that we are *not* looking for evidence to *prove* the Bible. We believe that the Bible is true. Therefore, we believe that God's Word is the best foundation for understanding *all* the science we discover in the world and in the universe.

RECOMMENDED RESOURCES:

CREATION MAGAZINE

Keep your family informed on the latest easy-to-understand evidences for creation and against evolution! This unique full-color family magazine gives God the glory, refutes evolution, and gives you the answers to defend your faith. Exciting articles and great witnessing material you won't find anywhere else! Includes a beautifully illustrated full-color children's section in every issue. Arrives every three months!

CHRISTIANITY FOR SKEPTICS

This updated classic answers key questions like: Does God exist? Why is there evil? Is the Bible the Word of God? What about other religions, including Islam and the New Age? It also contains cutting-edge material on design in nature and the Christian roots of science. Ideal to place in the hands of a skeptical friend, family member, or co-worker.

DINOSAURS! GOD'S FEARSOME AND FREAKY CREATIONS DVD

What does the Bible say about dinosaurs? You will be surprised how much! Fascinating evidence also fits the Bible's real history of the world from the beginning, and it includes these amazing creatures. See how we can use dinosaurs to teach age-old gospel truths. Both children and adults will love this entertaining and informative presentation.

For more information visit CREATION.com

CREATION.com

For more information on creation/evolution and Bible-science issues

AUSTRALIA
Creation Ministries International (Australia)
PO Box 4545
Eight Mile Plains, QLD 4113

Phone: (07) 3340 9888
Fax: (07) 3340 9889
ABN 31 010 120 304

CANADA
Creation Ministries International (Canada)
300 Mill St, Unit 7
Kitchener, ON N2M 5G8

Phone: (519) 746–7616
Orders & donations: 1-888-251-5360
Fax: (519) 746–7617

NEW ZEALAND
Creation Ministries International (NZ)
PO Box 39005
Howick, Auckland 2145

Phone/Fax: (09) 537 4818
A Registered Charitable Trust

SINGAPORE
Creation Ministries International (Singapore)
Clementi Central Post Office
PO Box 195
Singapore 911207

Phone: 9698 4292

SOUTH AFRICA
Creation Ministries International (SA)
PO Box 3349
Durbanville 7551

Phone: (021) 979 0107
Fax: (086) 519 0555

UK & Europe
Creation Ministries International (UK/Europe)
15 Station St,
Whetstone, Leicestershire, LE8 6JS

Phone: 0116-2848-999

USA
Creation Ministries International (USA)
PO Box 350,
Powder Springs, GA 30127

Phone: (800) 616-1264
Fax: (770) 439-9784

OTHER COUNTRIES
Creation Ministries International
PO Box 4545
Eight Mile Plains,
QLD 4113, Australia

Phone: +617 3340 9888
Fax: +617 3340 9889